BLOOM

Queer Fiction, Art, Poetry, & More

VOLUME 5, ISSUE 1

FALL 2013

BLOOM

ARTS IN BLOOM PROJECT, INC.
5482 WILSHIRE BLVD, #1616
LOS ANGELES, CA 90036
queerarts@gmail.com

EDITOR
Charles Flowers

POETRY EDITOR
Aaron Smith

FICTION EDITOR
Wesley Gibson

COVER ARTIST
"Rivulet" by Carol Pelletier
www.carolpelletier.net

MUSE
Konstantine Alexopoulos

BLOOM is a publication of Arts in Bloom Project, Inc. a nonprofit organization dedicated to queer writers and artists and their audiences.

EDITORIAL POLICY

BLOOM does not discriminate against the imagination. Gardeners must identify as Queer (LGBT), but the flora of their labor need not serve any preconceived notion of beauty. Peonies, sweet williams, ragweed, and gladioli—every shape and shade of blossom—are all welcome. Let the garden grow.

For submission guidelines, visit our website:
www.bloomliteraryjournal.org
www.facebook.com/bloomliteraryjournal

ISSN 1550-3291

CONTENTS

CONTENTS

NONFICTION

POETRY

The 2012 chapbook winners
are excerpted in the following pages.
All chapbooks can be ordered online at
www.bloomliteraryjournal.org

BLOOM Chapbook Series

POETRY

A Conversation with My Imaginary Daughter by James Cihlar,
selected by Lyrae Van Clief-Stefanon (2012)
Sky Never Sleeps by Jill Leininger,
selected by Mark Doty (2011)
Bruised Gospels by Phillip B. Williams,
selected by Minnie Bruce Pratt (2010)

FICTION

Fratricide by Alexis Stratton,
selected by Manuel Munoz (2012)
Ladies by A. Naomi Jackson,
selected by Nina Revoyr (2011)
A Small Uprising by Alicia Shandra Holmes,
selected by Richard McCann (2010)

NONFICTION

Tremolo by Julie Marie Wade,
selected by Bernard Cooper (2012)
States of Independence by Michael Klein,
selected by Rigoberto González (2011)

JULIE MARIE WADE

from "Tremolo"

THAT I HAVE STUDIED love through male lenses occurs to me now. *Agape*, the unconditional love of God for man, is the story of a son who did not fail his father—unlike the rest of us, selfish and unholy. Even *Eros*, the lesser love of humankind, is represented by a chubby, mischievous boy. Valentine's Day, though the province of lovers, though the holiday when manifestations of Eros are most likely to appear, celebrates a man's love for a woman, where love suggests passion, romance, and sexual desire.

The woman's story, I fear, has been occluded in this history of quest and conquer. Does she have dialogue? Will she initiate an act of longing? How will she know love, recognize and respond? Or is she always, at best, an adjudicator, evaluating the performance of men, the chivalry and championship of suitors, stumbling over each other in their rush to woo?

WHEN I WAS NINETEEN, twenty, a diligent college student— obsessed with abstraction, flirtatious with philosophy—I dissected love fiercely, squinted at it from every angle, toed the lip of the tub that might contain love, unsure or unwilling to descend. By this time, I had read Dickinson, Whitman, and Frost, dubbed them "lyric philosophers" in lieu of "poets," poetry seeming to me then too flimsy a term for such measured contemplation. Of course all the poets were dead, and all the philosophers, too—Kant and Mill, Russell and Rousseau—which left me wondering whether love would be given over to science for good. Oxytosin elation. Sympathetic and parasympathetic response. "Fight or flight"…which was just a fancy way of saying "love 'em or leave 'em."

Kirsten, who was my roommate and also my friend, cautioned against this growing reliance on science. "Everything you need to know about love is available to you through your own English major. Who do you like to read?"

"The Brontes, Austen some, Swift, Defoe…"

"Anything American? Anything from the here and now?"

I shrugged and looked up at my bookshelf, which was crowded with gilded texts that came as a set for Christmas. The look of these books had been more important at the time than their contents. "Usually I read whatever's put in front of me. Or I go to the library and pick something from the shelf at random."

Kirsten's brow bent, her bright eyes clouded. "I think people write love poems for a reason," she said, scanning the symmetrical tumult of her own shelves. "They aren't guide books. They don't come with instructions. But—" reaching for a slender white volume—"consider this a travel memoir from a place everyone wants to visit."

I took the book in my hands like the penitent I was, receiving my first communion. "My favorites," she said, "are 'The Night' and 'Rapture.' I think I'd like a portion of each read at my wedding."

THAT WAS ANOTHER THING: Kirsten wasn't merely an expert on love-texts; she had conducted her own field research. Nathan, the man she loved, was her one and only. They had met when she was seventeen in a Running Start community college math class. He painted houses and took photographs. He was older slightly, and calmer, with extraordinary eyes. Now she wore his ring on the fourth finger of her left hand—a small but unmistakable diamond. And this meant that she was promised, that love existed for her apart from and beyond its abstraction, like a creature crawled out of its shell.

E IGHT, NINE YEARS in the future, I think of that book again. I am living my own love story now, but curious as to how I arrived.

We reside in Ohio, which my West Coast imagination could not have envisioned all those years ago. What was this state but a placemat promise shaded gray or gold? An impossible place—yet I have loved and been loved here beyond abstraction.

The Barnesville Public Library has everything by Dickinson, Whitman, and Frost. The shelves are packed tight and precise with posthumous heroes, lyric philosophers. "I'm looking for a poet," I say. "Galway Kinnell."

"Never heard of him," the woman behind the desk replies. "Him?"

I nod, to clarify.

She shifts her weight and considers my face, then shakes the mouse beneath her mottled hand. "And the book you're looking for?"

"That's the trouble," I reply. "It's been a long time. I can't quite recall…I was hoping I'd know it when I saw it."

S OME NIGHTS KIRSTEN would read to me with the fortitude of a woman reciting her rosary. She knew the words in such a way that she did not require the page. Her effortless turning and her wandering eyes gave her quickly away.

I remember best the image of a man holding a woman from behind. They had just made love, a ritual so rife with passion and pleasure I could not believe it existed at all. Yet—in this Ohio state, this blissful Epilogue, he held her, her small body propped against his larger, his large body propped against the pillows or the wall, with light seeping in from morning. And he was described as the "big, folded wings of her," words I never forgot but turned over and over inside my mind, rotisserie of wonder and surprise.

The woman was an angel, of course. And the man a kind of angel too, watching over.

But some nights Kirsten didn't stay in the room. She packed her pillow and an overnight bag—or valise, as she was fond of saying. We were both writers. We hearkened to the thrill of words, particularly those that were strange or out-of-date. Antiquation could only increase their value.

When she went to Nathan's room, we never spoke about her destination, what acts of literature they might emulate beneath the dormitory sheets. She was gone, and I lay awake in my bunk with a book-light, envying those women of poems, their luxury of being seen so completely, their power to incite such desire.

ALEXIS STRATTON

from "Fratricide"

I.

THE SHUTTER CLICKED as the subway whooshed into the tunnel, blowing back bangs, ruffling bags, causing the waiting masses to step back. Click. Click.

One of the men nearby looked at her, her presence unexpected, unwanted.

She'd develop the photos later in her dark room, and his face would say the same thing, clear and captured there: *you do not belong here.*

HER PHOTO STUDIO in Seoul was bustling, a few of her students there working on computers along the walls. She'd been in Korea for five years, and her mom still asked every Christmas when she was moving back home. Melanie mostly ignored the question.

She wasn't planning to go back. She remembered telling her then-boyfriend Dimitri as much one night when they were lying in bed. He was an anthropologist, a researcher from Belgium. He liked to pretend he had insight into humanity. "Of course, you have a new life here. You have all you need right here." He pulled her close, skin touching skin, nose brushing against her hair.

IN ELEVATORS, she always stood in the back right corner, hands clasped in front of her, looking up at the numbers. People would get in and think she wasn't paying attention, but she catalogued each upon entry—clothes, shoes, hats, bags. Colors, framing, perspective, movements, shutter speeds. She made up thirty-second stories for each—just left by her boyfriend, up all night in Itaewon, abandoned as a child.

Every once in awhile, she snapped a shot. But only when no one was looking.

THE WATER WAS BOILING when they brought it out, a stew full of veggies and noodles, steam swirling up between them from a wide and shallow pot on the table. Her friend Mikyung had invited her to dinner at her family's restaurant on the Korean coast, a couple hours outside of Seoul. "My mother is a wonderful cook," Mikyung had said while they watched rice paddies zoom by outside the bus windows. Melanie pulled out her camera, took a shot of Mikyung, then one out the window, the Korean countryside so different from the bustle of the city.

When they got to the restaurant, Melanie paused for a moment at the aquarium tanks that lined the front—blue-black fish, shimmering eels, dancing octopi. Mikyung grabbed her hand and took her inside.

Mikyung's mom stood at the end of the table, watching the water boil. She'd spoken to Melanie in short bursts of Korean when they'd come in, but now her lips said nothing and her face was all worry and watching. In her gloved hands was a large plate with a small, live octopus, its tentacles hooking around the plate's edges. She gave an almost imperceptible nod, then bent over the low table. The octopus's legs clung to the plate as she lifted it with a pair of tongs and dropped it into the pot.

Melanie caught her breath, but Mikyung just kept talking about the lousy guy she was dating and how she was thinking of breaking up, how her mom had never liked him anyway, how she really wondered if she could make it with this photography thing, how she'd given her mom a framed photo as a gift and she'd really loved it—one of the ones she'd taken during Melanie's workshops.

The octopus was flailing in the water, arms reaching. It made no sound, was barely moving by the time Mikyung's mom cut off its legs, one by one.

WHAT TOLD HER she was like everybody else was the way no one looked at her on the subway. Only when she snapped a photo would a head turn or eyes meet. When she visited Korean towns outside of Seoul, she was surprised at the stares, sometimes pointing, boys and girls saying, "*Oeguk! Oeguk!*" But she couldn't help but smile then, to laugh as kids in school uniforms posed for the camera.

HE TOOK HER to Busan once on vacation. They went to the black pebble beaches, rocks scraping against her bare feet; to Busan Tower, where they climbed high above the city and watched the neon lights fizzle on at sunset; to Jagalchi Market, the largest fish market in Korea. The fish smell blanketed the city for blocks. They walked among the booths, the fresh catches piled in tubs, on tables, silvery scales glinting in the sun, the buckets almost overflowing with oysters and shellfish. Dried squid at the market were laid out on pallets, strung up on sticks, watched over by *ajumma*, old Korean ladies with bent backs and permed hair.

Later, they would stay in a motel that had mood lighting and a bed rimmed with black lights. He would tell her she was special, that he loved her. He would kiss her, bring her body close to his, but all she could think about was the booth full of giant pigs' heads, their black eyes staring out at her, the *ajumma* shooing away flies with bright, plastic fans.

THE FIRST TIME she stopped loving someone was under the sycamore tree. She wanted to love him, to believe that he loved her, that he would take care of her. But she knew she was wrong. She held a knife in her hand—one of her mom's good kitchen knives, the kind her mom yelled at them about when they accidentally ran them in the dishwasher.

She dug the blade into the tree's thin skin, made lines that made letters that made words, stabbed the metal into the soft inner flesh, scraped and dug and scraped again until the words were something big, something unbearable, and then again until they became unreadable, a jumble of slashes and jabs, until there was nothing left to interpret.The woman was an angel, of course. And the man a kind of angel too, watching over.

But some nights Kirsten didn't stay in the room. She packed her pillow and an overnight bag—or valise, as she was fond of saying. We were both writers. We hearkened to the thrill of words, particularly those that were strange or out-of-date. Antiquation could only increase their value.

When she went to Nathan's room, we never spoke about her destination, what acts of literature they might emulate beneath the dormitory sheets. She was gone, and I lay awake in my bunk with a book-light, envying those women of poems, their luxury of being seen so completely, their power to incite such desire.

JAMES CIHLAR

Coming Home after Teaching a Chaucer Class in which I Told the Students the Wife of Bath Is a Huge Drag Queen

Occasionally history takes a wrong turn,
leaving banks of time to be erased
by our latter selves. Today, in unofficial tribute to the Seventies,
I'm drinking Red Zinger, fondly remembering flairs and body shirts,
toasting my professors, who were the students of D.W. Robertson,
founder of exegetical criticism. The purring of a cat
is the engine of the house I share now with my husband,
the heart of the organism that is marriage.
Chaucer's pilgrims *quite* each other,
one story answering another. Feudalism's
treasured hierarchy dims in the background, while
millers, reeves, and wives negotiate in the foreground
to keep community running.
Even the provisional homes of the past
deserve their due. After an ancient break-up, a nap
on the foldout sofa, home from teaching freshman composition.
A canopy of maples outside the apartment window
flooding the room with gold shadow.
This shabby knows how to be chic.
The couple next door readying for bed naked
after a hard day's work, the curtains left carelessly open
across the narrow breezeway.
This is mine to profess:
Art means so much more to me than money, and
I woot best where wryngeth me my sho.

CELESTE GAINEY

a field guide to muff diving:

How we like it hard.
How the others like it I sometimes imagine.

But one thing to stop imagining, *please*—
is two chicks eating each other out.

That soggy old saw of lesbian sex
(mullets and the Indigo Girls)

is so Reagan-era eighties.
We may talk nice, look lipstick-sweet,

but the dykes I know
ball fists/strap on cocks

turn on backs/bellies
crack open cunts/lips/assholes—

bury the big hard-on—
blow it all to smithereens.

Why so much violence?
Why does pleasure carry pain inside?

Let's name it:
fury—

that's what two women breed in bed.
that's what we want/what we do/

feels like love.

more/less

more gay
than queer
more queer
than lesbian
less lesbian
than girl
more girl
than woman
less woman
than man
more boy
than bi
less bi
than butch
more butch
than dyke
more dyke
than trans
less trans
than faggot
more fag
than bulldagger
more bulldagger
than top
less top
than bottom
least top
no top
more bottom

less 's'
more 'm'
more bottom
more bottom
less homo
more sexual

Amor Fati

We wrestled in
the basement, drunk,

my head pressed
hard into the coarse,

blue rug, windows dark.
Upstairs,

my mother stood
at the stove. *Soon*,

my body seemed
to say, turning

under you. It was
1986: the fire

at Dupont Plaza, the
Human

Immunodeficiency
Virus, the

Challenger falling in
pieces over

the Atlantic. You
pinned me

there, bent
so close, I thought

we might
kiss, your shirt

stretched by
my long pull,

and I held on
with both fists.

Desire

My body was
its own

calamity. I locked
the door and stood

in the mirror to
consider what had

begun to change
against my will. This

was my father's razor, but
who was my father,

a man? And what
was that? The window looked

on a house, where the oldest son
spent most afternoons beneath

his car, the driveway strewn
with tools, his hands and shirt

smeared with grease. Once,
he called to me from inside

his garage, where I found
him leaning against

the far wall, his jeans
pulled down to his thighs.

Come closer, he said,
and I

didn't
but wanted to.

·

SALLY BELLEROSE

Sunflowers

THIS THE MOST BORING HOOD in America." Sixteen year old Ramon dribbles a basketball on the decaying driveway that belongs to the old ladies who live next door. He slips on a patch of ice on the mostly clear blacktop and rights himself. Ramon grins at his friend TJ as if not falling while he's dribbling is an accomplishment that might get him a spot on the varsity team. When TJ doesn't grin back, Ramon does his chicken dance. The boys' adidas are wet from walking in the snow.

TJ wags his head. "Hood? This ain't no hood. This is a Puerto Rican Dead End, ugly old white ladies in a falling down house on one end of the street, ugly young white ladies with ugly kids on the other end." TJ steals the ball and shoots at the hoop on the side of the driveway. "You spend half your life playing basketball and you still suck, man." TJ dunks the ball a second time. "Hoop ain't even got a net. Fucking embarrassing. This street…" He snarls at the street. "ReeCans up and down the middle, gringas on both ends. We're the filling in a white lady sandwich."

"ReeCans? Talk normal. Say Puerto Rican. Nobody says ReeCans."

"I just did." TJ makes his ugly face and tosses Ramon the ball.

Ramon dribbles. TJ and Ramon are tight, but TJ's got a lot of problems "at home" as the adjustment councilor with the big titties says to explain why he sometimes acts likes a dumb ass at school. She only sees him at school, when he goes to school. This morning TJ met Ramon at the bus stop, but TJ walked away when the bus arrived and Ramon followed. Mostly TJ is okay when it's just him and Ramon. Usually TJ saves his mean streak for jocks. He likes messing with punk jocks, which means messing with whatever team the punk is on. Weird because TJ would be on the basketball team, he's good enough, if his grades were better. Mostly, TJ goes after assholes who deserve it, but man there are a lot of assholes, you can get real messed up, waste your whole life going after assholes, especially assholes with teams to back them up.

Ramon wonders what he sees in TJ. Like right now, TJ's getting all strung out because Ramon's taking so long to shoot. One good thing about TJ, he likes to screw around, act a fool even, when he's not at home or at school. Today should be an okay day for TJ. He and Ramon are shooting baskets in the neighbor ladies' yard. Ramon's grandmother will make them maizena if they go over to her place. TJ likes to eat it slow and tease Ramon's grandmother about the two of them getting married and moving back to the island. But this morning TJ is acting like a ten inch prick.

Today TJ's not going near Ramon's grandmother or her maizena, if Ramon can help it.

"Well, you're the only one who says ReeCan, Little Man." Ramon is short and skinny. TJ is even shorter, but not as skinny as Ramon. And TJ is a lot stronger. "You getting your rag on, or what, TJ?" TJ's arms are roped with muscle, his chest broad for his size. Even under the two hoodies he's wearing anyone can see that TJ has a kick ass body. Both TJ's hoods are off. The head of the serpent that inks its way from his shoulder to the back of his thick neck and right up into the shaved edge of his hairline is visible.

Ramon shakes his head. With all that going for him TJ is still sensitive about being short.

TJ stares at Ramon who just keeps shaking his head until TJ wails the ball at Ramon's crotch. Finally, TJ smiles. His smile is butt- ugly today. Ramon turns sideways taking the blow on his hip. "Why are you doing me like this?" Ramon means to sound tough, but the hurt in his voice bleeds through. "Serious, what's your problem? Why you fucking with my manhood?"

"What manhood?"

Ramon slams the ball at TJ's chest. TJ catches it easily. Ramon turns, giving TJ the double finger as he walks away. When Ramon is all the way down the driveway TJ yells after him, "She's dead," like a threat or an insult, like it's Ramon's fault he doesn't know what the fuck TJ is talking about. Like Ramon killed whoever it is died.

Ramon freezes and asks without turning around, "Who?" Not TJ's mother. TJ wouldn't be playing basketball if it was his mother or one of his sisters. His grandmother in San Sebastian, maybe?

"The butch one," TJ says.

Ramon spins on his heels. "One of the old white ladies?" He nods at the house in front of them. "Jackie? We saw her yesterday."

"She had a heart attack." TJ squeezes the wet ball between his chapped hands. He looks like he might go for Ramon's crotch again, but puts the ball down on the driveway and sits on it.

Ramon walks back up the drive and crouches next to TJ. "We helped them tie that dead Christmas tree to the roof of their car yesterday." Ramon lives closer to the old ladies than TJ does. He can see them coming and going out their front door from his bedroom window. He points to their car which is parked at the curb.

"She died after we saw her, dumbass."

Ramon frowns. "That old lady is flat on her back, with the TV on, snoring like a beached whale." Ramon points his chin to the side of the house. "Right there in that window."

"Papi says she's dead."

"Your papi never says shit about anything." Ramon pulls the sides of his unzipped parka together and thinks about TJ's father. It's true, TJ's papi has next to nothing to say. When he bothers to talk, he says what needs to be said, bare minimum. The man could not be bothered to open his mouth to tell a lie. Ramon nods and says, "Shit. Only one white lady now."

"What have I been telling you?" TJ's eyes dart around. Ramon knows it's because he wants to run, but TJ is hanging on. Only his eyes are running. For now.

Ramon feels like crying, but TJ might get crazy for real if he does that. TJ loves that old lady. That's the truth. TJ spends a lot of time inside the old ladies' house when his father isn't home and his sisters go at it. He slept on the old ladies' couch just last week. TJ's the baby of the family and the only boy. Maybe that's why TJ gets crazy; all those women making all that noise, his papi gone half the time making money somehow, somewhere, barely saying a word when he's home.

The boys squat. TJ's ears are turning red. Ramon starts to tell him to pull up his hoodies, thinks better of it. Pulls the hood of his own parka up instead. Come to think of it the old lady, the dead one, is quiet like TJ's papi. The live one talks enough for them both. The dead one, Ramon wants to laugh, one of those horror movie laughs, the dead one will talk less than TJ's papi now. Jackie, her name is Jackie. The other one's name is Regina. Seems to Ramon, someone dies, you call them by their name. Someone's wife dies...Ramon can't finish the thought without barking out a laugh. The old ladies got married. What's he supposed to think about that?

TJ doesn't even flinch when Ramon laughs.

Ramon studies TJ while TJ studies a crack in the driveway. Ramon knows exactly how many nights TJ spends on the old ladies' couch. The whole neighborhood knows who sleeps where. They know that TJ's father slept in a third floor apartment with TJ's mother's ex best friend one time. They know Ramon's father kicked Ramon's brother Oscar out of the house for smoking marijuana in front of their little sister Evone and now Oscar lives with their grandmother and gets to eat her maizena every morning. Everybody knows every damn thing. But Ramon keeps his mouth shut about TJ staying with the old white ladies. Sometimes the only privacy you get is not having to talk about your own personal business.

"Only ever was one lady in that house," TJ finally says. He sounds like somebody else. Someone in a trance who might cry without having to punch out the person he cried in front of. His voice is soft, like when they walk in the woods behind the strip mall.

Ramon knows what TJ is saying. Jackie was barely female, buzz cut, men's pants, work boots, on an old lady. A really old lady. "What's going to happen to her, the pretty one?"

"Pretty?" TJ is back to being a dick. "She's poor. She's old. She's white. She's a dyke. Pick any two and it don't add up to pretty."

"You got a white girlfriend," Ramon says. "She ain't old," he concedes. Reconsiders. "But she's poor." He runs a finger along the crack in the blacktop wondering how TJ, with his shit for personality, got a pretty girlfriend. Must be his body. He wonders what the girlfriend lets TJ do. "This is why you've been ugly all morning?"

"How am I supposed to know what's going to happen to the pretty one?" TJ looks like he might spit on Ramon. Not that he would. Probably not. He spit on Ramon's sneaker one time. TJ's shoulder starts twitching like it does when he's trying not to hit someone or trying not to cry. Ramon has seen him cry, but not since TJ's favorite cousin got killed by a hit and run and even then TJ crying meant TJ crazy after he stopped crying. Ramon can see the shoulder moving right through the layers of hoodies. He pretends he doesn't see TJ's arm spazzing.

TJ jumps up. "Let's go see."

"See what?"

"If she's in there, sitting on her chair like a beached whale, like you said. Maybe Papi got it wrong. People on this street." TJ's voice lifts with the thought of how wrong people on this street can be. "You see an ambulance? You hear sirens?" TJ's excited like he hit on the essential point that's going to save the old butch white lady from being dead. Like his papi, maybe this one time, carried a rumor without checking it out, without making sure it was true before it came out his mouth.

"Sirens every night." Ramon thinks a minute. Maybe TJ has a point. "You hear them, same as me, but never on this street, hardly ever." He stops, yeah, maybe TJ is right. "No ambulance next door, not last night."

TJ sprints around to the side of the house, stops dead in his tracks, stands with his back against the faded clapboard a few feet from the window. Ramon stands shoulder to shoulder with TJ. If she's not dead, Jackie should be sleeping on the ratty chair inside the house at this time of the morning, not five feet from the window.

"Look inside," TJ hisses. He crouches and hugs his knees, his butt against the house.

Ramon would tell him that the mold on the clapboard is going to rub off on to his jeans, but TJ would be disgusted if he knew Ramon even thinks about this stupid shit.

"You look inside." He slides down next to TJ. "She was your girlfriend." Ramon winces at his own remark. He didn't mean to say was, didn't mean to disrespect the dead, not with TJ looking so messed up, his arm twitching, his chest heaving like he ran a mile. Ramon is afraid of looking and finding an empty chair, too. "TV ain't on."

"How do you know?" TJ stands up. "The window is closed. How do you know the TV ain't on?" TJ's voice is a loud squeak.

Ramon shakes his head. "She likes the TV on loud, man." TJ knows this. They've spent enough time slumped against the side of this house by this window to know you can tell if the TV is in on or not even with the window closed. Even on a cold day they can catch the score of a Patriot's game by listening near the window. "Let's get out of here. Your girlfriend is dead." This time Ramon says girlfriend and dead on purpose. He figures if he can piss TJ off by repeating the shit about Jackie being TJ's dead girlfriend TJ will go just a little crazy and they can fight instead of looking in the damn window, not seeing Jackie sitting on the chair, and having TJ go full blown crazy.

"Shut up fool." TJ punches Ramon in the biceps but there's no muscle behind the hit. He stops breathing and listens hard.

There is noise coming through the screen window. Not snoring, not the TV. Whimpering. Ramon leans forward on the tips of his sneakers so his stick-out Obama ears can catch the sound. "Jackie," he whispers.

TJ shakes his head. "Regina." TJ, on his feet, squints through the window. His hand shades his eyes from the glare that bounces from the snow to the glass.

Ramon stands behind TJ, puts a hand on his shoulder. They stare in at Regina.

Regina, who handed them cookies like they were little kids, just yesterday or maybe the day before. She's sitting on Jackie's chair. They see her in side view. Between the screen and the fact that there is no light on in the room, the boys can't see her very well. They can tell it's her though. She's on the edge of the seat, staring straight ahead, an old lady zombie making a sound that's getting louder or maybe just sounds louder because the boys are listening so hard. She's so close that if the window was open and they leaned way in they could touch her.

The pane barely rattles as TJ puts a hand flat against the window, but Regina cocks her head responding to the sound.

They watch Regina's slow-mo move as her head swivels in their direction. They watch her frown as she fights with the sash to unlock and raise the window. They watch her close her eyes and bite her lip as she manages to move the stuck screen. Ramon wants to yell, "Never mind the fucking screen." Something is happening in his chest, like somebody shoved a fist in and is squeezing his lungs, maybe his heart. It hurts bad.

When the screen is finally up the old lady says, "Oh, TJ. Oh, Ramon."

TJ and Regina stare at each other. TJ's mouth is open. It makes him look stupid. Ramon feels like he's doing something bad, watching the old lady's sad face and TJ's open mouth. Regina looks older by the second. TJ's hoodie gets wet in the front. Ramon wonders if TJ knows he's crying. He wants to run, but he can't leave TJ.

"Remember the time Jackie caught you peeing on the rhododendron in the back yard?" Regina says. "And that bouquet of sunflowers you picked for her. She still has those, on a vase on our dresser, all dried up." She smiles, a far-off looking smile that scares Ramon. "Ten years of dust, all the seeds fell out a long time ago." She sighs. "I tossed them in the trash, but she pulled them out."

Ramon takes a step back. Shut up about the fucking dead sunflowers, he wants to yell, TJ doesn't know the difference between a rhododendron and an oak tree.

"You were about six years old," Regina says, almost happy. "So cute."

TJ nods and his fists curl. Ramon wonders if TJ remembers it was him, Ramon, and not TJ who got caught pissing on the rhododendron. Ramon can't remember if it was him or TJ who gave Jackie the sunflowers. TJ's fists clench and uncurl. He is fighting his hands so they won't try to put themselves through something.

Ramon stares at Regina wondering if she'll have to move. Where's TJ going to go when he can't hack it at home if she moves? He can't stay with Ramon. Ramon's father doesn't understand that some people live in places they have to get out of once in a while.

Regina leans closer and puts her fingertips on TJ's cheek. The pain in Ramon's chest pokes at him. He sees Regina's face clearly, her hair uncombed, the wrinkles deep. "She loved you. She would never say it, wouldn't want to embarrass you or herself, but I will." Regina's lips are dry. She usually has pink lips and cheeks. Her face is all the same grey today. Her voice sounds younger than usual, a girl's voice coming out of an old lady.

Ramon tries to breathe the knotted fist out of his chest. The old butch one is dead. He has known people who died, young people. He held a baby once, a little girl who lived right down the street, held her while her mother picked up the shit that fell out of her purse. A few weeks later that baby died. Ramon kind of liked holding her. She smelled good, but he didn't panic when that baby died. His cousin died. Ramon tries to calm himself by thinking of all the people he knows who died and all the times he didn't panic. He sucks in a big breath and holds it, a trick his father taught him. If Ramon doesn't stay cool he can't help TJ stay cool. Old people, Ramon reminds himself, that's what they do, they die. But Jackie, somehow he thought Jackie would wait until TJ got better. Who's going to help Ramon help TJ get better now? He holds his jaw to stop his chin from shaking. Ramon closes his eyes, hoping TJ and Regina keep staring at each other for a minute so he can think of something to do to get them all out this, some way to get the pain out of his chest, but all he can think about is their future. His and TJ's.

Ramon has been holding back visions of their future for a long time. They're only sixteen so, if neither of them dies young, there's a lot of future pressing hard, breaking through his thoughts at the wrong times. He sees them, him and TJ next week or next month, maybe tomorrow or later this afternoon, after TJ stops falling apart and comes back together, and he will, TJ will fall apart and he will come back together, maybe crazier than before, but he will come back, he always does. Ramon tries, but he can't hold back his worst thought - TJ losing the fight to keep his fists down, going after who-ever is closest. That's what Ramon is most afraid of - TJ not able to keep his fists at his sides until he finds a punk who deserves them. TJ wailing on whoever is closest.

Ramon wonders when his mom and the rest of the neighbor ladies will come with rice and beans and cake and mass cards. The old dykes have lived here since before the boys were born. The neighbor ladies will turn out for them.

He realizes his mom doesn't know yet, none of the ladies know. TJ's papi wanted TJ to know first. So TJ could pay his respects before everyone else got there. He tugs on TJ's hoodie. TJ shakes him off.

"Say sorry, say sorry to Regina." Ramon can't remember using her name before and he says it like a punk now, in a high nervous voice. "Then we gotta go TJ. Sorry for your loss." Ramon wishes he didn't have to look at Regina when he says this. If Jackie was TJ's old lady girlfriend, Regina is Ramon's. "I'm sorry. Real sorry. We gotta go." He grabs a piece of TJ's arm when he yanks at the hoodie this time.

"Get off me," TJ growls.

"She loved you too, Ramon." Regina is wearing some kind of a nightgown that she forgot to tie at the neck. The pepperoni skin on her upper chest shows. Ramon cries, not hard, he thinks he can stop. "But TJ…" She puts a spotty hand over her heart.

TJ grips the window sill, turns on his heels and runs.

RAMON FOLLOWS HIM. He's never been as fast or as strong as TJ, but Ramon catches up and tackles him on the front lawn. They roll over each other, bodies slamming together, hanging on like they'll drown if either one of them lets go. Then there's the moment that both boys long for and dread, when their eyes meet, when the rage and fear hang in the air and everything stops.

"TJ. I don't want to fight you. I don't want you to hurt…" Ramon voice is too tender for either boy to bear, "anybody."

"Get off me," TJ shrieks. The boys are on their knees. Ramon locks his arms around TJ's chest. TJ struggles, but he's fighting against too much, he collapses, an old trick to make Ramon put down his guard for a second while TJ rallies then busts out of the hold Ramon has on him. But Ramon knows this trick and before it happens, Ramon puts his head on TJ's shoulder and kisses TJ neck softly, right there on the frozen lawn next door to Ramon's house, right there in the neighborhood, not out in the fringe of woods a mile from here, where no one has ever found them, or only the one close call when TJ waved around a comb that the other boys thought was a blade, making the punks scatter and TJ laugh like a maniac.

Ramon knows kissing TJ's neck is wrong, the wrong thing to do in the old ladies' yard with the butch one dead and the almost pretty one crying in her too big nightgown. Everything is wrong. Ramon pulls his lips away, holds TJ just tight enough so he won't slip to the ground, taking what he can get, one last time he thinks, but then he thinks one last time every time he kisses TJ. Ramon holds on and waits for TJ to bust out and start swinging. They both wait for TJ to explode. For a long moment TJ stays limp and spent in Ramon's arms.

TJ doesn't burst out. Ramon stops holding him and says, "Sit up, man." Ramon puts his arm over TJ's shoulder, like Ramon's father does to Ramon once in a while. "Fuck all of this, TJ." He means fuck one old white lady being dead and the other one looking tired as death and talking in a little girl voice. He means fuck TJ going to see his pretty white girlfriend after he and TJ have sex behind a tree near the strip mall. He means fuck TJ being crazy. "Jackie's dead. I'm here, man, but I'm done with crazy." He knows it's the wrong thing to say to calm TJ. He knows it is exactly the wrong time to say it. He knows he and TJ will both die some day and if he doesn't say it now he never will. "Done babysitting." Ramon wipes the tears off his face with the sleeve of his parka. "Done fighting you, TJ."

TJ's broad back and shoulders stiffen. "What about fucking me? You done with that, too?"

Ramon takes his arm away. The question hangs there. Ramon pulls his head back. The boys stare each other down. They have never talked about what they do in the woods. Ramon thought TJ put it out of his mind as soon as it was over. He thinks what they do in the trees behind the strip mall is part of why TJ is crazy, but it can't be all of why TJ is crazy, because he was crazy enough before they started going to the mall.

"If I have to be," Ramon says.

TJ wipes the tears and snot on his hoodie. "I got your back too." His voice is close to calm.

Ramon nods, almost smiles because he's not sure if TJ means in the neighborhood and at school or in the woods when he lets Ramon cry on his shoulder without giving him shit about it.

"We should do something," Ramon says. "Flowers or some shit like that for Jackie. She liked those big yellow ones. The ones that grow by their back fence."

"Fucking sunflowers," TJ says. "Why you pretending you don't know they're called sunflowers."

DANEZ SMITH

raw

I've spent all day trying to come
            up with a metaphor for barebacking.\
I've tried face against abrupt winter,
            sockless feet against velvet floors,
punching a warm beast with paper skin;
            none of them work. I don't want to talk
about the risk because I don't want to
            think about risk. miss me with that
chatter about what I know is wrong. I know
            the bones I could become, I know the story
& the other one too, how people disappeared
            mid-sentence in the 80's, how NYC became
a haunted bowl of dust. I know the monster
            waiting to pounce my blood, but I wasn't in
my right mind, I was barely in my body at all.

DANEZ SMITH

land & sky & water & cum

aren't we an anomaly

of kicked up dirt & water?
        body, just uppity wind,

pressure system who doesn't
        know when to leave. I am warm

front knocked up against
        brick wall, his body is fresh

from the Canadian hills,
        there is a tornado in my mouth

ruining all my teeth, leaving
        nothing behind but plaque

& pant. I should say this
        all happens in the alley

behind our hardware job,
        I should say he is forty

& I am not. how old am I?
        at the time I still had a curfew,

know that. but back to his body,
        his rank Hanes, overgrown

pubis, sour foreskin, this is
        the word *natural* at its best.

what is semen but condensed cloud,
        the body's recipe for lightning?

what is the ass but a canyon
        begging the tongue to jump?

what is the taint but hail,
        that odd child of the sky?

my mouth is busy asking,
        storm of his flesh in front of me,

I cast out my tongue like a key
        strung to a kite,

wait for thunder.

Identity

A finger of clay
kneaded by enormous thumbs.

No harm done. Everything you were
is all still here. This blob

could be a head, a career,
a dog with a scarf around its neck,

a fedora being sat on, a pickled herring, a pipe-cleaner man,
a geisha smiling under a lantern, a grave someone is rubbing,

an accessory to a crime, a wet seal nosing the bit of clay
that was supposed to be your life.

Still a Guy (early transition)

> "The day is about to come, put on your body."
> Cesar Vallejo, "The miserable"

You had big dreams of being a little girl, and then you dreamt you
    were a woman.
You felt your spark ignite, your skin open inward like a folding door
to reveal a better skin, more luminous, more even,
a margin from which life could finally work its way in.

You felt like history being made
in a world not yet discovered,
a terminated world that picked itself up,
shook the ruin out of its hair

and became a woman. You dreamed
the day was about to come, an ecstatic body
you were putting on, grinning and dressed to the nines,
stepping out into the brisk black wind of time,

just born and suddenly old, with keys and a car and a license
to try on every color, build a house, vibrate
on subterranean trains,
hand out compliments.

You critique yourself as you walk by,
your father's son in a thrift-store skirt,
lashes thickened but still a guy
beneath the breasts that stretch your sweater,

floating above and looking down
on women who are real, telling yourself
you're better, truly, than everyone you know
you're not as good as,

layering on extra necklaces, signing up for correspondence courses
in how to tell the truth, how to talk to guys
without feeling like a guy, how to talk to women
without wondering when to blink your eyes,

what to do when your body rides up
and reveals you squirming inside,
an insect in a jar. How to become a woman, day after day,
and not hate what you are.

CHARLES JENSEN

An Object Lesson

The place, then: small high school, rural town. More cows than students, more barns than families. More endlessness. From any point in town, you could look out and see for miles—fields, pastures, the lines of tall maples and oaks dividing property, stuck into the ground like slim pins in a road map. The thousand variants of green—emerald, Kelly, chartreuse, hunter, clover, avocado, olive, pine, sea foam, shamrock—and the visual textures of the fields—burlap before planting, corduroy during tilling, velvet before harvest. Things were planted to be grown, grown to be discarded. It was here I met Mr. Nash and wrecked his life, wrecked my own.

I could smell Mr. Nash minutes after he'd walked through the hallway, the cafeteria, near the office. Like encountering a ghost. The smell went directly to my head. My knees bent involuntarily and I'd make as though I were steadying myself from a stumble, which was true.

My job, now: same as his. Educator of young minds. Mr. Nash taught physical education, but I train the brain—really, the heart. I train the eye to see images in words, identify themes, pull out symbols and tropes and clichés. I read to my students the way Rick never would have. But he shaped our bodies as carefully as a sculptor. His tools, not awls, were drills and games. With me, his hands.

I was sixteen. Old enough to know better and young enough not to care. The impulsiveness of youth: feel now, think later. Suffer later. Regret later. Putting off until tomorrow what I should have considered up front. I was unpopular, alone in high school. I had very little to lose. And I was as full of want as an empty wallet. I had the potential to hold something of value.

Mr. Nash looked at me—it was the first time anybody had really looked at me—and said, *Call me Rick.*

Mr. McDaniel, my student Andrew says, his hand touching my waist without enough hesitation or uncertainty. His hand moving backwards, following my belt.

I wasn't there for Rick's last day. The administration, the principal, encouraged me to stay home as the other "children," he said, would be full of talk, most of it what I didn't need to hear. I stayed home a week. I ignored the phone, making my parents take the calls from teachers, other parents, even the obscene calls of my classmates, where all they'd hear was breathing, a dirty word, an accusation against me. I gave them a punishment equal to my own, my own rediscovered solitude.

Andrew's breath at my ear. What he whispers when we are alone.

The shape of Rick's shirtless chest in the locker room, changing after his morning workout in our weight room. I saw him blurred through the cloudy fiberglass windows of his small office. The scent of his cologne drifted out into the room where I pulled on my gym shorts, unlaced and laced my shoes with pointed precision. Lost in his scent. Like being held close to his body.

Andrew's eager hand shooting into the air like a warning shot, ready to answer the question I've posed before I've fully posed the question. In the dim half-light of the rainy afternoon, his skin veils over with a light blue tinge, his lips purpling, his eyes like an owl's—wide, dark, knowing.

Rick has become a ghost.

I told my father only because he already knew. My telling was a performance. Distinct from a confession, which holds shame.

Rick's mustache—almost orange—unfurled across his lip like a pair of wings.

When he told me to do push ups, I did as many as I could. Then I did ten more. I'd wake up the next morning unable to raise my arms, to pick up a stack of books. But his face afterward: he believed I could. So I could.

Andrew's favorite book is *The Catcher in the Rye*, followed by *The Stand*. He is, first and foremost, an adolescent, I tell myself. What's an adolescent, then? Adult desires without adult moderation. When I first started tutoring him after school, I suspected nothing. I thought he was a well-intentioned junior struggling to do well. Later, I saw these layers crack and chip away, a sheet of ice coating a windshield. After four weeks, I noticed he did not make the same errors in his writing. The errors were random, inconsistent—one week he'd confuse their and there, another he'd misuse the serial comma. That he was cutting and pasting these samples from the Internet I learned once it was too late.

I reported Rick not because I didn't want him, but because no one wanted him to want me.

It's a question of perspective, like a house built to fool the eye: you stand on one end of the hall and see a small doorway in the distance. You walk into the room, a ramp, crouching under the sloping ceiling, to suddenly stand near the door, half your size. The view from sixteen to twenty-five doesn't seem so long until you look backwards.

There are three ages high school students perceive of the adults around them. One is seventy. Another is forty. The last is twenty-five. There is no in between. What's in between, to them, is invisible.

We are so close I feel the heat of his body invading mine.

Someone saw us. Saw us drive away from school, or zip through town as rain fell like tobacco spit onto the roads and crooked, half-hearted sidewalks. Saw his taillights lingering in the rain outside my house where my parents were surely sitting down to dinner—where my plate, empty, was already a kind of confession. Or they saw what came next—my face, his hands—

The principal asked to see me. He explained what he already knew. I lowered my head.

In adulthood I would realize he knew nothing—just suspicion, just rumor.

A bluff.

You wake up one day and there you are, twenty-five. Wearing a tie to work every day—a tie you only learned to knot a year ago when your grandfather died. You go to work where the age you are is so old, the students you teach think you can't remember what it's like to be their age.

Rick was twenty-five that year. Twenty-five, first teaching job, still ripe with the blush of his youth. His body responsive to diet and exercise in all the right ways. His savings account constantly zeroing out with impulse purchases, spontaneous trips to Vegas, New York, Seattle.

A new stereo. Maybe that's not him at all—maybe I'm making this about me. But what did I know of adulthood then? I imagined beer in the refrigerator, popcorn and Cap'n Crunch for dinner, a futon in the living room that folded down for make out sessions where the new stereo murmured sweet, seductive tones from its stubbled speakers. Rick was like me. But Rick was not like me. Before the year was over, I knew the taste and texture of his lips, his mustache pressed against my face, the almost pleading force of his breath pressing into me.

Andrew can make no such claim.

After Rick left, people stopped bothering to whisper. I spent a good portion of every school day making new bruises—shoved into lockers, knocked to the ground, tripped on the basketball court. I was smacked, pushed from behind, pushed from the front. Once I was spit on by a senior, his saliva hitting me square on the mouth, getting inside me like a long distance kiss. I was pantsed during an assembly, my underwear exposed to all my classmates and teachers, and no one moved to help me. I bent over, pulled my pants up, looked at the blank marble faces of the administration, and went home.

It was the only time I cried for him. Rick, I said my pillow. The next words—*I'm sorry*—I couldn't speak.

Andrew brings me a mix CD, dropping it off before first period. He enters my classroom in a pressed white shirt, belted khakis, walks like he's king of the jungle. This early I keep my lights off—fluorescents for too long give me migraine headaches. The tables and chairs wear their housecoats of shadow behind his tall, lean body. His hair moves gently, tousled by a breeze somehow connected only to him. *Here,* he says, his mouth baring his teeth in a smile. I take it from him. To refuse would suggest too much: to accept is a way of saying *your gift is insignificant enough to take.* I nod in thanks as the first bell rings. He winks, gives me a cocky salute, and jump-jogs out into the hall.

I turn the CD case over where he's listed the songs. The titles, when read from beginning to end, create a kind of narrative—"all night long," "touch me," "you are mine," etc. I have not explained to him the role of subtlety in art, how suggestion is often more powerful than confession—how holding something back is enough if you can convince your audience what you have is worth getting.

Therapists have convinced me to say I am not responsible for what happened with Rick. They taught me to say, *I am the victim*. And it is true. I am the victim of my own adolescence.

The place, now: suburban high school populated with kids who own their own cars, have multiple iPods, text while walking, text while eating, text while talking to the person they're texting. We have computers in classrooms, Wi-Fi throughout the school, and email addresses for students and faculty. The median age of this city drops to sixteen during daylight hours. Where the adults go, I can't say for sure—to their jobs in the city, I suppose. Their children they leave behind like dogs, unleashed and hungry. It is my job to keep them occupied until dark.

Andrew's parents attend Parent-Teacher Night. He shows them off proudly, like he's done such a good job raising them. And he has: they hover around him like two small birds, constantly pollinating his flower with praise, hugs, attention. I shake his dad's hand, introducing myself. *I'm Mr. McDaniel*, I say, perpetuating the false formality of our high school context. In two hours, in a bar down the street, sharing a pint and a game of darts, I'd be Mike. His mother, taking good care of her looks, calls herself Shane, a name Andrew warned me she'd invented. She has a beautiful body, stands just an inch or two below Andrew, doesn't say much. His father, where Andrew gets his looks, has a retired model's confidence and lack of arrogance, as if he knows his best years are behind him, but he's still had those years. They are nice people. They don't deserve Andrew. They deserve someone more like me.

But we play the hands we are dealt. Andrew, doing his part, bluffs and bluffs and bluffs.

Is this okay? It was what I said when the light in Rick's eyes changed. I saw something come down like a sign in a window, and after that, he looked at me with his real eyes. Which I liked so much better. They turned me from a child into an adult, matching up who I was outside with who I believed I was inside.

Andrew's hand on mine with the certainty of a mousetrap.

My face in the hard, corded trunk of Rick's neck, drowning in cologne.

The long drive home from school, where I confirm all of the things I did right in deflecting Andrew's advances. A shorter list of my failures. An even shorter list of my transgressions. A beer bottle on the counter and everything it has ever known making its way into me.

Teenagers will tell you everything worth happening happens after school. The hallways empty, quiet. Muffled sounds of a girl crying echoing against the cold ceramic tile of the bathroom. The clack of heels across the tile floors, the click-click of a big institutional door closing one last time. The whistling of the janitor drowning out the shush of his mopping.

Imagine: what is happening right now in the music department's practice rooms.

Imagine: what the library's web browsers discover about themselves, what they can do.

Imagine: a confused new life appears in the body of a girl in a parked car.

Imagine: the smell of the boy toking on a joint beneath the football bleachers, his breath and smoke indistinguishable in the cold autumn air.

Imagine: this teacher, telling you this story, uncertain of how it ends.

Imagine: this teacher, years ago, filling a teacher's mouth with his own lies.

Imagine: years later, the man I am contending with the boy I was.

Rick drove a Camaro, what I once heard Ms. Trueblood, chatting in the teacher's lounge with the door open, as a "penis car." Naturally, it was red, had a CD player in the stereo deck. If I came to school early enough, I could sometimes watch him roll in, driving a little too fast, riding the speed bumps with recklessness, the kind of recklessness that drew me to him. If I stood under the pine trees clustered near the east doors of the school, guarded by their heavy arms, he would walk within fifteen feet of me, not knowing I was there. It was my dream: to be a ghost behind him, following him through his day, to be where he was when he stripped away the mask of Mr. Nash and became fully himself. That was the real fantasy: to see into his life, to be in his life.

Andrew comes late to class and expects to be forgiven. Or to be punished, so that he can beg to be forgiven. He walks to his seat like his feet barely touch the ground, a smile across his face so big it almost touches either ear. His eyes crinkle shut like a Shar-Pei when he does this. I ignore his cockiness because it's what he expects me to do. I go on with my lecture about *A Tale of Two Cities*, discussing how the horrors of revolution are never fully understood until much, much later.

I ask myself now if I would have been different back then if I'd had a friend, a good friend I could have talked to. In adulthood, I picture a girl: slightly heavy, not unattractive but without either the money or the interest in making herself pretty, eager to be liked. Those eager to be liked always find themselves friends with the people who hate themselves—a kind of adolescent yin-and-yang. Her name is Jennifer, the most common girl name from the year I was born. As it was, my class had seven of them—one Jennifer for every thirteen students. After school one day, we'd walk through town to the gas station where we'd buy Funyuns, Chee-tos, and Slim Jims, forcing it all down with Diet Cokes as we'd sit by the town lake with our shoes off, our toes burrowing into the sand like little crabs.

I have a secret, I'd tell her.

Tell me, she'd say.

It's a big one, I'd say, taunting her.

Mi-KULL! Just tell me. Chomp, chomp, chomp.

Mr. Nash is my boyfriend, I'd say, the words vomiting out of my mouth with their own purpose. We'd laugh about it. We'd eat our Chee-tos and we wouldn't get fat.

When sunset came, I'd hear the roar of Rick's Camaro in the distance and know I was loved.

When Andrew approaches me after class, he tells me his mother thinks I am a "good looking guy." He says it like that, with quotes around it. This is because he either doesn't believe it or because he cannot unbelieve it. He's made the other students vanish with his lingering. I sit behind my desk, barricaded, and speak with cool detachment. *If you show up late again, I'm putting you in detention.* I place my hands on the desk to prove their uselessness.

Detention? he parrots in a sinister tone. He leans over the desk, placing his hands near mine. His eyes squeeze shut above his grin. *Promise?*

Andrew's hand on mine with the certainty of a mousetrap.

In the aftermath of my transgression, I withdrew even further into myself. I stopped speaking to my parents, although the conversations we'd had before then were nothing for the record books. I wore a lot of black. I took up smoking cigarettes while I sat in the window of my room, staying up all night long, listening for the sound of a car engine that might be Rick's. Would he come for me? Did he forgive me? Did I deserve to be loved? I filled a blank journal with poems about my feelings, poems about Rick's body, poems about the feelings Rick's body gave me. My mother slipped envelopes of cash under the door when it became clear I refused to answer. I only came out once they'd gone to bed, their operatic snoring the closest thing to automotive acceleration I was ever going to hear again.

Andrew's breath at my ear, warm. He whispers his words to me. His breath smells like peppermint and sour patch kids. We are so close I feel the heat of his body invading mine, trying to convince me of something I refuse to hear. Then his hand is on my waist, moving backward. I feel myself get hard and immediately grow sickened by my own arousal, but am unable to turn it off. I lean backward slowly, the movement almost hurting me. I see his whole face now, pleading, desperate.

I realize: *I am the one in control.*

Would Rick be absolved if I explained my car broke down after school, that it was growing dark, that it began to rain, that he was one of the last teachers to leave that day, that his Camaro's open door released the thumping beats of a new No Doubt song, that his clothes were slightly damp from an afterschool run around the track in the humid spring air, that I went to him willingly, that I seduced him, that I put my face up to his cheek as we idled in the stormy dark outside my house, that I leaned over and put my lips on his, that I even went as far as opening his lips with my tongue, that his mustache against my mouth burned after a minute of his kissing, that I put my hand on his thigh and pulled his foot off the brake?

Imagine: you are driving that car.

Imagine: you are that boy.

Imagine: one of you asks, *Is this okay?* And it is.

Andrew suffers from none of my own debilitating uncertainty. Although he is not "out" at school, he cares little for what other students think of him. Rather than isolate him, this trait makes him immensely, immensely popular. In the cafeteria, his table bulges with teenagers. There he sits in the center, completely at ease, completely owning the attention of everyone around him. When I do lunch duty, I catch his glances. He wants me to see how loved he is. He wants me to see how easily he could have someone else. He wants me to see this and know he still chooses me.

Though I desired Rick, though I dreamed of him at night, though I was haunted by his smell and the shape of his body and the way his voice boomed through the gymnasium as I ran laps for him, I hated myself. I hated my too-skinny body, like a clock with six extra gears all working against telling time. I hated my hair, my skin prone to acne, my inability to make nonsense small talk with people in my classes, my stupid clothes that never fit me longer than one washing. I willed myself into translucence, but the effect was only social: no one saw me. Only Rick did, and then, not for what I really was. I was like a foggy window through which the weather always appears to rain.

I drive a Hyundai Accent: what my students call "a Teachermobile."

No one in my life now knows the story of Rick. I live in a different state now, having attended a far away university where I knew no classmate would follow me, where I could dig my feet deep into the soil and root down. There was some news coverage at the time—in that decade, if students weren't sleeping with teachers, they were shooting them—but its reach was purely regional and so, about a year after I last saw him, my connection to Rick went as deep underground as I could will it. My parents and I made peace with ourselves and, over time, they accepted me because we all seemed to agree to forget that year with its dark revelations and collateral damage.

Andrew's soft voice, asking, *Can I do this?* I pull myself back, step out of his half-embrace. His hand falls lamely to his side where it hangs like a broken branch.

No, I say, straightening my tie.

Not like this. Not here.

With Rick in the Camaro, our bodies craning like two lampposts over the gearshift and emergency brake. The radio bleating out sad love songs again and again. The storm tapping its army of fingers against the roof, insistent. *Is this okay?* I ask. With Rick, my face buried in the hard, corded trunk of his neck, drowning in his scent. The hair on his legs coarse and curled under my hand, gripping the tensing muscles in his calf, his thigh. His hands purposefully holding the armrest, the gearshift. A lightning flash we saw behind our eyelids; the thunder, its echo, barreled towards us across the empty field where he parked, the fields only suggesting the riffling rows of corn that would appear there in a few weeks. The wings of his mustache spreading across my face, my chin, my neck. His tongue wide and flat, pushing into my mouth. I took him in. I leaned forward.

His hand reaching across that invisible line that separated what happened to him from what he committed.

Call me Rick, he said.

The thunder broke again, dropping its noise over the budding fields as though startled. I didn't hear anything after that.

My Middle Ages

We are fairly sure there was sunlight,
nights when I did not sleep on the floor,
wake with half a bottle of Southern Comfort.
The taste of cherry I could sweat out with a run.
My virtues: I don't have hangovers, I can talk
to my husband five states away without slurring
my words, I can flirt without leaving
home or hosting. I can afford better liquor.
Jack Daniels, a midnight streaming of *Grown Ups* –
no hyphen, just maturing prepositions – before
I teach, before I tell students that this business
of breaks between light and dark and light
is bankrupt. That one should never say
whenever I want to stop drinking, I will
just stop. That we no longer call them
the Dark Ages.

Fingers, Hands, Hips, & Lips

Dainty like tines, fingers,
like teapot spouts pouring hot
shame into my parents' cup
of diminishing kindness.

Hands flourish, exclaiming the world's
festive beyond grief.

Hands on hips, feathering palms, akimbo,
right tilt of my sisters' conqueror stance.
Unsuitable for basketball, they curl
but never succumb into fists

—unlike my father's—

rather, lift the hips to horse-
rump pageant stomps.

Deliver lips into songs.
Piaf-sparrowing, Imelda karaoke.
High pitches & giggles & squeals

much to my parents' bursting discomfitures.

Yet fork tines spear the meat.
My Maria Clara graces fan the flames,
heavenly mock-diva tendencies.

Nonetheless: my disparaged humming body,

which father forces arms
to their sides, soldierly;
subdues into a boxed-in crate.

The stifling, as with

my verbose uppity mouth clamped
by mother's fleshy forceps.

Lips squeezed to fatty pucker
as if to extract a mollusk
from a conch shell.

Boys

There is no loneliness like theirs
Bearers of the burdens of legacy
Superheroes monsters Legos and blue
Boys are their mothers' true love
Prone to territorial pissing
Caterpillars between their legs
Drones boars and stallions
They tear small animals
Into pieces bound to set things
On fire wake-up in cold sweat
Castration and lupine nightmares
Boys look to the sky for escape
Fly dangerously close to the sun
Comic books spinning wheels a swim at sea
Boys kiss one another, and feel anger shame
Each slides a hand down the front of a woman
Continent in their imagination
Fail miserably there
Play the fool overcompensate
Spread out their legs to distant landscapes
Prodigal sons grow coarse
Rhinoceros skin a tusk while at it
Warring war cultures
Steel mortar plastic and wood
Pallbearers miners butchers and priests
Boys refuse to dance when the dancing matters
Destined to break their daughters' hearts
Their hair cascade like ribbons in barbershops
Mirroring eyes well up with clarity and remorse
Adam in the apple lodged in the throat

Prostate of the idyllic body
In search of their mothers boys will
Love many women and men
Musk oil the lot of their
Forefathers fathers
Mankind's foreskin

Father/Son Dance

I am the child that crunched up near the tire grease and spectated
    intently
and delighted in the music of your voice, the nonsense rhymes
of chrome&cog mechanics

& when I jubilantly said I'd grow up to be Daddy, the
    miscommunication made you dream
of blueprints and lava soap, and crescent wrenches laid out like
    piano keys

but what I wanted
was feet to fit your boots,
complete with hairy toes encased in steel

& not the endless meaningless blood,
in gushes and torrents and nauseous waves,
that was at first a shock, a day of tears, but then subsided
into another dull ache of resentment, bone-deep, chromosomal.

You could have passed on to me
the tribal drumbeat XY chant. Instead
my cells hum white noise, one syllable like the Hindu om, ringing
    like trapped water in my ears.

The peyote god has granted me a different dance but
there's no shining desert beyond the chrome of the kitchen when,
a decade later, we stand at the sink, arms newly scrubbed of grease

and I spit it up finally and your lips go thin and disappear
into your beard. I know our Anglican world won't abide
any of that silly vision business, or drumbeat dancing, or especially
      swapping

and so the demon Lady Luck clamps down her teeth,
tightening her grip right where it hurts.

I don't know how long we lay there on the meticulous white bed that was not our bed, in the apartment that was our apartment but not our apartment.

HILARY ZAID

The Neighbors

WHEN THEY'D BEEN TOGETHER long enough to consider having the child they both knew they never wanted, Trisha and June bought a cat. Not a pound cat: a cat-food-commercial, fluffy cat, a brand name cat, a "Norwegian Forest Cat," a cat whose thick white chest matched their sofas and rugs, a cat who sat after dinner in June's lap crunching triangular snacks that stank of shrimp, mewing with contentment in a way I found distinctly menacing. Because they'd rather die than be considered precious, they named the cat Toonces, after the Saturday Night Live skit, "Toonces, the driving cat," the one where the cat always winds up behind the wheel, careening over a cliff. June liked to sink her long, manicured nails into Toonces's thick fur and sing the theme song to Toonces's greedy purrs.

Naturally, when Trisha and June took their annual trip to Venice and needed someone to look after Toonces, Francine and I were the ones they asked.

The weekend before they left, Trisha led us into the guest bedroom where, we'd discovered, June slept by herself. ("Oh, God!" June's voice had dropped two octaves; her chin retracted into her neck in shock at the suggestion of regular spooning, "We never *sleep* together unless we have sex!") "Ellen, if something happens," Trisha instructed me, pulling a lined wicker basket out from under the bed, "come right over before my parents get here and make this disappear." Trisha settled a plump hand on the top of the basket, whose contents were concealed by a red and white checked cloth, wholesome as a picnic basket.

"What is it?" I blinked, unthinking.

"Our porn collection," Trisha smiled, a wide, thin-lipped Cheshire grin.

T HE SUNDAY AFTER THEY LEFT, we found the apartment across the hall preternaturally quiet, and flooded with light off Lake Merritt, brilliant platinum light our street-facing windows never got. We pulled the blinds half-closed and tiptoed through the living room, calling, "Toonces! Toonces!" in overly cheerful voices. June was gone and Toonces, I suspected, was going to be pissed.

"She's probably hiding," Francine suggested, when no sign of the white-chested fur ball turned up—no sign, that is, except for the big, turd-like sludge on the white carpet in front of the couch. "What is that?" I gagged.

"Hairball," Francine answered, peeking into the bedroom. "Here, kitty!"

I peered closer at the moist *vomitus* and nearly retched.

"Come on," Francine chided me. "I'll clean it up. Pussy," she mumbled. She pushed past me into the little kitchen. "You wash out the food dish and put in the wet food. Just half a can."

Francine went to work on the living room carpet with a wad of paper towels, a plastic shopping bag and a big white bottle of Nature's Miracle. A preschool teacher at the Jewish Community Center, Francine is efficient with unpleasantness, like a nurse. This makes her especially good at the parts of working with really little kids she refers to, sarcastically, in certain company, as "wiping."

W HEN TRISHA'S SALARY first broke the six figure mark, June threw a formal party, complete with caviar *blinis* and silver bowls of bite-sized $100,000 bars, at the Women's Cultural Arts Building, in the big red ballroom where, June claimed, Gertrude Stein and Alice B. Toklas had once danced together. Francine and I were skirting the crowd, looking very busy with our drinks as we always did at Trisha and June's events, when we overheard one of Trisha's clients, a man in a bold, hibiscus-printed silk tie, boasting "they cut the guest list under 100k. Smart. It's all about who you associate with." He leapt backwards out of the path of a falling *blini*, as the sour cream hit the floor with a thick *splat*.

"We did consider it," June acknowledged, blankly, in a stage whisper in the garden, "but we'd never hold *you two* to the income line! You're in a different category!" We were, after all, The Neighbors. Which was how she introduced us to Trisha's parents.

Trisha's mother, her face puckered into a polite, inquiring smile, turned to me, "Trisha tells me you're a Jewess?" The word felt strangely animal, like *lioness*, or *tigress*. I spent every day transcribing the memories of the Jews who had survived Hitler; I was familiar with the animal motif, if not in this part of the 20th century, not in this part of the world. I just blinked.

Comfortably lubricated, pink and platinum Mrs. Hendricks swiveled affably to Francine: "And what do you do, dear?"

Francine, whom I would never hesitate to call My Better Half and mean it, might have had one and a half mimosas too many. She quipped without so much as a sly smile: "I wipe."

Mrs. Hendricks, all the muscles in her stout body encased in her red linen suit, froze, her face a struggle not to let pure puzzlement overtake good breeding. "Oh?" Trisha's mother swept her head from one side to the other in a gesture meant to convey: "How fascinating!"

Francine nodded: "I wipe hands. And noses. And butts." I touched Francine's elbow, but Francine bobbed her head forward, shrugged her shoulders confidentially. "*Tushes*," she corrected herself, to convey that she, too, was a Jewess. "And tables. And chairs. I suppose," she mused, "you could say I'm a Renaissance wiper."

D ON'T FORGET the litter box," I reminded Francine. Actually, fishing the perfect half-eggs of solidified kitty litter out of the box with the big slotted spoon seemed less offensive at that moment than handling the glistening, gelatinous brown stew of fish-stinking cat food. Still, all the jobs were dirty ones. We'd get to whisk the little fishing rod with the bell and the green feathers across the carpet once all the shit work was done.

I scooped the double bowl from its fleur-de-lys placemat on the floor, flicked a soggy, star-shaped kibble into the garbage disposal, noticed a dirty glass left in the sink and realized I was thirsty. I opened the cupboard above my head where Trisha and June kept all their tumblers. "Jesus," I muttered. I pulled glass after glass out of the cupboard, each one, in the light of the half-curtained window that overlooked the little half-curtained kitchen on the fifth floor of the building next door, filmed milky white.

"So, wash one," Francine told me, tying up the end of the plastic bag in which she had stuffed her wad of paper toweling and cat vomit. I hunted around the edges of the sink, where Trisha and June had tucked a brown glass Salviati vase out of Toonces's path, and where I also found the tattered remains of the sponge, a limp moss of yellow-green whose treaded surface had been worn to bits of synthetic pill, all its honeycomb of spongeness squashed flat. I picked it up with two fingers. This was no longer an object that could make other objects clean. I wondered if it could even hold soap. Shifting the sponge gingerly to my other hand, I had nearly reached the tap when the smell hit me. A noxious blast of mold, fetid damp and ancient food, the ghost of garlic cloves and breakfast eggs, Cheerios gone fat and blurry in leftover milk. I nearly fainted. I turned my head away, my eyes shut tight and blurted "This stinks to bloody hell," an expression I'd picked up from Trisha.

"It's a sponge," practical Francine started, "how bad can—" But as she stepped towards the kitchen, she caught a whiff of the thing, and Francine, who had just scraped cat vomit off the living room rug with her bare hands, dry heaved, a single, groaning retch that brought her hands to her face. "Christ…" she murmured, her face pale. We stared at each other across the gold-flecked Formica countertop.

"What should I do with it?"

"Throw it away!"

"They won't have a sponge."

"We'll get them a new one."

"What will we tell them?"

"That their sponge was disgusting."

"Really?"

Once, I had gone into the guest bedroom to retrieve a book June had borrowed. June, who was just coming out of the bathroom, caught me in the hall just as I was shutting the door; she rushed me with the terrifying glare of a pissed-off witch. Francine and I had fled the apartment, June in hot pursuit: "You need to go. Now!" It wasn't a moment we joked about.

Francine considered the sponge still dangling from my fingers. "We'd better put it back."

Like a spy erasing evidence of a break-in, I set the sponge delicately back into its wet nest on the edge of the sink, then scrubbed my hands raw with the last of the dish soap.

M AYBE IT HAS SENTIMENTAL value," Francine suggested. We were sitting kitty-corner on the white sofa and the big white chair, flicking the green feather idly back and forth for Toonces, who had not emerged from her hiding place.

The shivers had stopped shimmying my shoulders, but the sponge had started to seem safely funny. "Maybe it's their first sponge," I said, "and they can't bear to throw it out."

Francine's hair spilled over the back of the big white chair. She'd tucked her legs up under her.

"Maybe it's an heirloom," I went on, trailing the feather along the rug. I sat on the couch, leaning forward, my knees at the edge of the glass coffee table. "Maybe June's parents brought it to this country from Korea. Maybe it's their last ancestral possession." I was joking. Sort of. My own grandparents and great grandparents, fleeing pogroms at the turn of the last century, inconveniently, had brought nothing. Across the room, June's celadon bowl winked, a huge green eye, under its bright museum spot.

June's celadon bowl *was* an heirloom, and, according to June, an antique as well. At a tiny cocktail party we'd dropped in on at the apartment, I'd heard June tell Trisha's mother that the small green tea bowl, incised with fish and waves, came through her family from the twelfth century Koryo dynasty. "Have you ever had it appraised?" Mrs. Hendricks had cocked her head, her thin lips the perfect model of Trisha's. June had pulled her head in, aghast, her eyes bulging behind her thick glasses; she tried to mask it with politesse: "Oh, my goodness. No. My grandmother's mother hid this vase among her linen after the assassination of Empress Myeongseong. When my mother came to America, she carried the bowl still wrapped in my great-grandmother's *heoritti*."

I didn't envy June her heirloom bowl, exactly. I envied her the history. (We were 20th century American Jews. In the high tide of Diaspora, the sandy footprints of our *shtetl* history had been washed entirely away. Even our mother tongue, within the span of a generation, we'd managed to shed.) June knew about her mother, and her mother's mother, and her mother before that. She knew their names and their places in the family line. (Though it was June, with her seven-generation family tree, who cautioned against romanticizing the past. "If we lived back then, we'd have married men, given birth to seven children, and, if we hadn't already died in childbirth, be dead by the time we were thirty.'")

"Maybe they're saving that sponge for *Antiques Roadshow*."

At the mention of *Roadshow*, Francine brightened. "They got it at the neighbor's yard sale and just," she flung her fingers wide, "neglected it all these years by the kitchen sink, never suspecting that it's an authentic relic of Colonial Virginia—"

"The sponge Martha Washington used to scrub George's chamber pot—"

"Yes!" Francine coughed out a little bark of laughter, "and saved by Thomas Jefferson's mistress—"

"—the slave—"

"—and then, tragically, lost to history—"

"—but uniquely identifiable by its eighteenth century flora."

Francine fixed me with a deadpan stare. "Do you have any idea how much this sponge is worth today?" She wore the earnest demeanor of the *Roadshow* appraiser, truth on the threshold.

This was the moment for tremendous expectation masked with tremendous naiveté. "I really couldn't…" I gestured in mock, faked cluelessness.

"That sponge," Francine intoned, "is worth ten thousand dollars."

I threw my hands up to my face.

The sudden jerk on the cat toy I was holding sent the green feather arcing from the coffee table to the wall, and Toonces darted in, ears back, eyes narrowed to green slits.

"Here, Toonces," Francine cajoled, stretching out her fingers.

Toonces pressed by my legs, nonchalantly allowing Francine's fingers to drag through her thick fur. I jerked the feather-on-a-pole up and down, trying to entice her. Toonces, ignoring the feather, leapt onto the coffee table, pushed a *Martha Stewart Living* to the floor, and spread herself out on the glass in a corona of white fur. Like everything else in their apartment, the cat was tidy, expensive, glamorous.

I dragged the feather under the table, slowly, back and forth, trying to catch Toonces's attention through the glass. "You like that stuff," I ventured, considering Francine's true passion for the *Roadshow*. "Antiques." I waved my hand toward the celadon bowl.

"It's fun," Francine shrugged. "It's history," she added, meaning, I should like it, too.

"Not just the old stuff," I wrinkled my nose. "All this stuff." I swept my arm around the room, taking in the big, stuffed chairs, the tall bookshelves lined with glossy, coffee-table books, the Limoges box on the side table.

"It's okay," Francine considered Trisha and June's living room. "Not exactly my style."

"But, I mean," I cleared my throat, "you want those kinds of things." I couldn't quite bring myself to say what it was that I wanted to say.

"You mean, nice things?"

I was an oral historian at a small non-profit. Francine was a pre-school teacher. I shrugged, self-conscious. Francine wanted a pair of real cowboy boots. She knew the brand names of hats. "Yeah."

Toonces flicked her tail back and forth against the table.

"Sure," Francine conceded.

I nodded, depressed. My desk was made of particle board.

I stared down at the feather, which I trailed back and forth, back and forth beneath the table, its green plume shining like a cheap jewel.

"Don't you?" Francine stood up and picked the celadon bowl gingerly off its pedestal; she balanced it lightly on the tips of her fingers, rotating it slowly, like a globe. "Want nice things?" When I didn't answer, she nodded toward the bowl, "Not fancy things. Just a nice house with nice things. Like a real couch." Our lumpy futon couch, a relic of my graduate student days, had become a point of contention more than once.

"I guess," I shrugged. "Yeah."

Toonces flicked her tail against the glass with a resounding thump. Her ears lay flat. She refused to look at either of us.

I frowned, "But I don't need expensive things. I don't need to collect paintings," I looked around. Above the mantle hung an acrylic painting of pink dots, covered in Lucite, painted over with yellow blobs that looked to me like pollen, or antibodies, a painting of an allergy. Trisha had bought it for June at a gallery in the city. "This is definitely going to appreciate when the artist dies," Trisha had told us, "and he's in his 70s." "I don't need coffee table books and blown glass vases."

Francine set the antique bowl down in front of me on the table. "I don't either. I'm not the one who grew up in a house full of antiques, remember?"

"Francine—" I hated having my parents' wealth held against me, as if it were my fault, as if it were something that made the distance between us unbridgeable. "Your mother had a French country dining table." I loved her mother's table, as a matter of fact. It was so unlike my mother's style; sitting at that table on Sunday nights at the Jaffes' was one of the things that made me feel like I could actually become a part of their family. "It's not like—" Without warning, Toonces leapt from the table, grabbed my leg with both front claws, piercing the fabric of my pants, and bit hard.

"Shit!" I screamed.

Before the word had even cleared my throat, Toonces was back on the coffee table. Her fur, pressed flat against the glass, spread around Toonces like a halo, her ears flat back, head serene, eyes narrow.

I pulled up the leg of my pants. Two ruler-straight lines of flesh had just begun to bead up scarlet stitches of blood where Toonces's claws had pierced my jeans. Bright jewels of blood rose in a semi-circle where she'd bitten my shin.

Francine stuffed her hand into her mouth; she was laughing hysterically. "I think she knows you don't like her!" she coughed.

"This cat is crazy!" I barked, stunned. "It attacked me!"

"Ellen," Francine chided me, "You must have flicked the wand up your leg."

"She *attacked* me," I insisted. Francine shook her head.

I sat back down in the overstuffed white chair and tucked my legs up under me, wary. Toonces stared, steadfast, into the distance, flicking her tail.

"You know it's not the same," Francine argued, going back to the French country dining table. "My parents have a house; they have decent things, some nice things, even. But they don't drive BMWs, they don't go to Europe twice a year, they don't have a second home. They don't even have a timeshare. But they feel like they have enough." Francine worried the green feather between her fingers.

I wanted to believe she would be happy with what her parents had. "I guess," I answered. "But," I pressed her, "don't you think you actually want more?" Wasn't that how it went? I had had everything, and I didn't care. But Francine, who hadn't grown up with antiques, watched *Antiques Roadshow*; she almost certainly wanted more.

Right?

Francine turned to me. "You're sounding a lot like Trisha right now." Francine raised her palms to the antique wooden moldings, the fatal, framed litho of histamines. Trisha had told us she and June were looking at houses in Rockridge. *Houses*, as in more than one house. One to live in and one to flip.

My mouth dropped open. "That's low," I protested. "You know I don't think life is like Monopoly," I countered. "You know I don't care about how many houses and how many hotels I end up with." I wasn't protesting too much. I spent every day interviewing Survivors; I know how easily it can all be stripped away.

Francine's curls bobbed. "I know," she conceded softly. "But maybe," she chewed at the cuticle around her index finger; Francine looked back up at me, "Maybe you just assume, you know, that you'll eventually, automatically have all that stuff, because you grew up with it. Maybe you don't even know you want it. Maybe," Francine shook her hair back and looked at me piercingly, as if I were receding before her eyes, "maybe you'll be the one who's disappointed."

Before I could think of what to say, Toonces leapt from the table, reared up on her thickly furred hind legs, grabbed Francine's shin, leaned in and bit hard. Then, just as quickly as she'd come, she darted off, an evil spirit vanished into the master bath. Clutching her leg, Francine looked up, aghast. "Jesus Christ!" In an instant, she'd vanished behind the closing door of the guest bedroom, holed up against the cat.

I found Francine sitting on the white bedspread, examining her shin, which was punctuated with the same Morse code of feline aggression as mine. "Did you see that? That cat attacked me!"

I had no interest, right then, in making the obvious point. I just wanted to get the hell out of there. But when I cracked the bedroom door, I discovered the pacing sentry of Toonces, flicking her tail, barring escape. In our rush to escape the cat, we'd cornered ourselves. "Shit."

"We'll wait her out," Francine assured me. "She's evil, but she's easily bored." I wondered if Francine was thinking of June and her crazy alter ego, but I was too shaken to joke. I told myself it was because of the bloody puncture to my shin, but it was the sharpness of Francine's accusation that kept stinging me back to the question of money and things, and which one of us wanted them, which one of us would disappoint the other. If Francine was right, if the craving for money was like cat scratch fever, then I'd already been infected, no matter how much I protested. I stole a glance at Francine, who had sunk into the 400 percale white-on-white duvet, her red curls spread out around her head like a crown, and thought, *She's the one who wants stuff.* But that petty thought, too, failed to console. Were Francine and I really so different? "Come here," Francine patted the pillow next to her head. "This isn't so bad, is it?" I let the goose down pillow envelop my head. Was it? I found myself succumbing, as a cloud of lavender etherized my niggling thoughts and a mass of feather pillows smothered the voice of frugal protest down to a murmur of pleasure. I don't know how long we lay there on the meticulous white bed that was not our bed, in the apartment that was our apartment but not our apartment. Outside in the hall, Toonces purred menacingly. She paced with heavy tread.

We must have fallen asleep. When I opened my eyes, Francine was rummaging through bedside drawers. "Just looking for a Band-aid," she tapped her leg, unconvincingly. *Really?* I scanned the white walls, a horrible black drip painting behind us, certain that June could see us with some terrible, third eye and would track us down and kill us for ravaging her inner sanctum. Yet, Francine was the moral compass of this relationship, and she seemed perfectly at ease. *Okay*, I thought. *What's wrong with indulging a little harmless curiosity?* After all, we were doing them a favor, and we were trapped. Emboldened by Francine's boldness, I fingered the magazines on the bedside table (*Martha Stewart Wedding* scandalized by a handful of *People*) and, remembering the basket of porn, went fishing under the bed, where my fingers hit cardboard.

It wasn't the wicker basket, but an archival box, the kind you might use for photos. I scented the whiff of history. *Sepia photos of June's great grandmother?* I wondered, hungry for story. *Birth certificates stamped with a Korean chop?* To have money was one thing. To have a fortune in documents about her people and her mother land was something else. While Francine moved to the closet at the foot of the bed, I opened the box with the relish of pure, unadulterated greed.

The contents, a stack of cancelled checks, couldn't have disappointed me more. I thumbed through the pale, money-scented slips, scrawled and stamped checks in the pastel and greens and golds of banking tender, like a pile of fallen leaves, all of them addressed to *K + H Properties*, the same company to which we addressed our rent. Why did Trisha and June have a stash of checks addressed to our landlords? Were these seemingly innocent, social climbing lesbians a pair of thieves, embezzlers, a real life Thelma and Lousie? I shot a quick glance at Francine, who was rifling through dry cleaning bags in June's closet. Before I could think to accuse them, realization grabbed me in its daggered claws. I flipped through the checks madly. There it was, printed on the rainbow flag-printed check Francine had ordered from HRC: our check, written to *K + H Properties*. Months and months of them. Years worth of them. *K + H. Kim + Hendricks*. They weren't The Neighbors. They were The Landlords. To people like them, this pile of checks was porn.

"Francine—" I started up from the bed, my legs shaking with terror. If this was what Francine wanted –a life played like Monopoly, a life like the one that my father had built—then I could never compete. If Francine knew how far I fell short, did it mean she would leave me?

Francine whipped her head toward me, her freckled face blanched. *Did she know?* Her mouth fell open, but she couldn't speak. Instead, she stepped aside. At her feet, revealed behind the curtain of dresses Francine had parted, were boots, the kind of boots Francine had been envying, saving for, hinting at for months. She tossed one to me. The black leather nearly melted in my hands. Boots like the ones Francine wanted, only better. Newer. Imported. I sniffed the leather. Italian. I tossed the boot back to Francine, who set it back in its place, along with the other fifty pairs in the closet, all of them identical, none of them worn. I felt sheepish. My mother, too, had a shoe closet. But this was something else.

Francine looked shocked, a stricken slackness around the mouth I mistook at first for envy, until her cheeks flushed the crimson I recognized as high indignation. "Can you fucking *believe* this?" she breathed. She pulled the plastic curtain of dry cleaned clothes shut over the shoes. "Let's get out of here. I feel like I'm going to suffocate." She was disgusted, I realized, a welter of joy rising in my chest.

"The cat—" I protested. But Francine didn't care. She'd seen the true wages of excess, and she wanted none of it. And I couldn't have loved her more.

I shoved the box of checks under the bed; Francine closed the closet and grabbed the door knob with white knuckles. "Ready?" Before the word was out of her mouth, Francine had flung open the bedroom door. We threw ourselves in a panicked dash across the living room, our eyes scanning frantically for white on white. "The bowl!" I cried. Francine and I had left the heirloom bowl out on the table. If we left it there, Toonces would probably knock it to the floor or—worse—June would see that we'd been handling it. I hesitated, balancing the specter of the cat, poised to leap from above, to dig its feline claws into my scalp, against the angry ghost of June, ready to smash me over the head with her Grandmother's bowl. "Just run!" Francine yelled. Chasing the brilliant flame that was Francine's flying hair, I saw us fleeing this apartment that was like our apartment but not our apartment, escaping this parallel life that was not our life.

I leapt for the door as Francine flung it open. We jumped into the hall and collapsed against it to the door's echoing slam down the dark stairwell.

"Let's go home." To our museum reproduction posters, she meant, to our one, shared bedroom, our own clean sponge. Francine and I clutched each other, grateful and humbled, proud and fierce, as we tumbled on wobbling legs through our own front door.

ELEANOR LERMAN

Grief

Think. Is it because it seemed so easy for the beauties
          who got here first
and now their journey from our wrecked and desperate coast
          is a story that's been scripted for the movies?
Because they write each other's names upon
          golden pages
and stay inside all afternoon, resting
          "in languid repose"?
True, the wind from the dry hills stirs the curtains
but it's still a hot day because the sun feels like
          it has to serve these people
It thinks bitterly about their swimming pools

Is it because you once believed it would be possible
          to live here without work or money?
That old-fashioned queers would buy you drinks
in the holy name of how you used to be good looking
and share their medications because your grief has a
          name and size and number?
Because it can be seen from so far away?
That means nothing. Everyone suffers in this movie:
Civilizations rise and fall. It's all on tape

So think. Think hard. There must be something
          that you wanted, badly
because you flew here in a plane, crossed each
          indivisible mile
with that creature of yours locked up in the hold

Or is it that you'll travel anywhere these days
just for the chance to set it free?

ELAINE SEXTON

Short Back & Sides

The reason it doesn't hurt
when it's cut is

it's dead, the biologist said,
brushing her dead bangs,

the color of bark,
back from her dead

eyebrows reaching up,
surprised we didn't

know this already. The sushi
came just then,

the wait staff with hair
cut severely,

uniformly straight. The rain
pounced the pavement

agressively, plashing
back, knocking the plate glass

where we sat sipping sake.
For the first time in months

a smile stretched my lips
till they hurt

and I reached for your
dead grey locks,

curling with impunity
in the humidity

exposing the buds of your
ears. So queer,

the Super Cuts mentality
under discussion.

$20.00. Butch
or femme. *Why spend more*

on something that's dead
you said. *Hair:*

the sexual organ
that shows, someone

read. No wonder we pay.
We love our stylists,

clinging, dependent.
My best friend,

someone said.
How we cried

over a bad color
or cut, evocative locks

severed from their nests.
Our scalps let them go.

Dead anyway, right?
Why should we care?

The temperature rose.
Dead strands,

bleached, and gelled,
blown into place,

hugged one Upper
East Side head

turner, then the next,
gingerly passsing by.

Someone shook
an umbrella,

someone shook her head.

ROBIN LIPPINCOTT

Piece of My Heart

L IKE ME, SHE CAME from a small Southern town—hers was Port Arthur, so far southeast Texas that it's almost Louisi-ana—mine was Lake Mary, Florida, so central that it's just about the middle of nowhere. I recognized my town, and hers, in such films as "Bonnie and Clyde," and later, "The Last Picture Show"—the quiet, dusty streets, the flat landscape, the scattered one and two story buildings, and the sense that time had passed it by.

Over the years, many people—on learning where I'm from—have insisted that Florida isn't really the South, but they just don't know; they're thinking about the more exotic part of the state, of cities like Miami and West Palm Beach. Where I grew up (Central Florida) and when I grew up there (the 1960s), was the Deep South; remember, this was before that confection known as Disney World changed the area forever.

Although I'm talking about the 1960s in Lake Mary, it might as well have been the 1950s or even the 40s by the look of things, and by the oppressive, conventional mentality of many of the townsfolk. The center of town was a gas station!

And then there was me—a budding artist of some stripe, medium yet to be determined—tending toward fat like the rest of my family: to say that I was a misfit or an outcast in Lake Mary would be an understatement.

The same was true for Janis. "They laughed me out of class, out of town, and out of the state, man," is how she put it during an interview on "The Dick Cavett Show."

But for years before that, she'd had to endure. She was overweight in her teens, and she had a bad case of acne. To be female and not conventionally pretty in the South back then (if not still), was—well, not pretty, almost as bad as a boy being labeled a sissy. Janis was called a "pig" and a "freak" during high school, and in college at the University of Texas she was voted "The Ugliest Man on Campus." She studied art there and started hanging out with other misfits, listening to Bessie Smith and Leadbelly, and singing the blues in bars.

School was hell for me, too—from grades one through twelve. The harassment, both verbal and physical, was incessant. And home wasn't much better: for the first eighteen years of my life, Mama ran a daycare center out of our house, so there were always twenty to thirty other kids around to whom she was paid to pay attention. My sole ally on the home front was the black woman Mama had hired to help out with the daycare and a few chores around the house, Adeline McKenzie. Otherwise, I had nowhere to go, nowhere to run and nowhere to hide, as the song goes. And so I turned inward.

My bedroom was my sanctuary, a reflection of the created world I retreated to every chance I got. I papered the walls and eventually the ceiling, too, with posters, until scant wall space remained. I can't even recall now what all the posters were of, but I do remember a large, blown-up still from "Bonnie and Clyde." And there were several posters of Janis, too.

It must have been the release of the album "Cheap Thrills" by Big Brother and the Holding Company, the band Janis was a member of at the time, and the subsequent radio airplay of "Piece of My Heart," that first brought her to my attention. Just as I would recognize my hometown in "Bonnie and Clyde" and, later in "The Last Picture Show," I immediately found something of myself in Janis. She was singing her pain and her anger, singing the blues, raw and real, but it was the universal pain of the bullied, too, of misfits, and she was screaming for attention.

The opening scene of "Bonnie and Clyde" shows a naked Faye Dunaway as Bonnie Parker applying lipstick as she looks at herself in the mirror. She sighs heavily, walks over and collapses on her bed, hits at the bedpost with her fists in frustration: she is bored, tired, weary, sick to death of this dull, small-town life. She does not want to have to keep on doing the same old thing over and over again, day-in and day-out, like everybody else seems to do in this godforsaken town—because she is not like everybody else. She feels as though she'll scream, or die if she has to continue to live this life one moment longer. Or was I projecting?

Clyde was Bonnie's way out, and Janis, in many ways, was mine. Just as Bonnie's life was never the same after meeting Clyde, mine couldn't possibly go back to what it had been once I'd experienced Janis in all of her honesty, intelligence, beauty and freedom. Because of Janis, I felt less alone, and I also, finally, felt some sense of hope (however small)—that it might just be possible for me to escape the daily torment for being who I was, to move on, and eventually to express myself in some way. Because of Janis, I was able to own my anger, and I was also able to get in touch with my sexuality: during high school I broke from the rest of my family and dropped the excess weight that I had carried for so long; I also let my naturally curly hair grow out and stopped trying to tame or straighten it, so that I was the only white kid with an Afro at Seminole High School. My classmates' predictable response was, "Did you get your finger stuck in an electric socket?"

But there were still too many years—agonizing seconds, minutes, hours, days, weeks and months—to be endured between 1968 and when I finally left Lake Mary for good, and those were the worst years, too. High school was a source of daily torment to me, and I skipped classes as often as I could, which was never often enough. The harassment seemed to increase in proportion to the rising testosterone levels of my male classmates (gym was a particular nightmare), and it also became increasingly physical: rare was the day that I escaped unscathed.

But Janis was there with me now and I knew it. In the high school cafeteria, somewhat miraculously to me, two of her songs were on the jukebox—"Piece of My Heart," of course, and the flip side, "Turtle Blues." Listening to Janis on the jukebox in the high school cafeteria became yet another coping strategy for me, of which I had devised as many as I possibly could.

Because of Janis, I had finally grown a set of balls (she gave me strength and courage), and I cannot begin to describe the pleasure I took in forcing my classmates to listen to her every day at lunchtime. Every once in a while I'd play "Piece of My Heart," but more often I selected "Turtle Blues," not only because it wasn't as well known, but also and very specifically because, like Janis, I also felt like a turtle, sitting there in my hardened shell. But even more, I chose it because of its opening lines:

—I'm a mean, mean woman
And I don't mean no one man, no good, no

I desperately wanted to send the message that I, too, was mean, and that I meant them, especially the boys who were continually taunting and harassing and abusing me, no good whatsoever.

The keen pleasure I experienced listening to Janis on the jukebox in the high school cafeteria only increased once my classmates began immediately acknowledging my selection with an audible, collective moan, as Janis launched into her vocal assault, and I, in my mind, at least, launched into mine:

—I'm a mean, mean woman....
And I don't mean no one man, no good, no

Until one day, one of the jocks got smart, walked over to the jukebox while "Turtle Blues" was playing, and kicked it—sending the needle skidding across the record, all the way to the end.

Janis's death from an accidental overdose of heroin was devastating to me. I don't think it's hyperbolic to say that I lost my best friend the day she died. I learned of her death on the radio that morning before school; in fact, it was the news that I woke up to, since at the time the radio turning on served as my alarm clock. At first, still in that watery place between sleep and waking, I thought it was just part of a nightmare I was having, which in fact it was—the one that dominated my waking life, the one I lived every day. Once I was fully awake and the sad reality of Janis's death began to sink in, I told Mama that I didn't want to go to school, that I didn't feel well—because by then, after everything I'd been through, I had a pretty good inkling of what lay in store for me. Always tone deaf to anything that pertained to the spirit, once Mama had made up her mind about something, she was undeterred, dug in her heels, and forced me to go to school anyway, regardless of how I felt.

Of course my instincts were right, as they usually are, for what did I encounter that day at school but classmate after classmate coming up to me, casually happening to mention the news of Janis's death, and then laughing right in my face. At which point the nascent warrior inside me growled in my belly.

But rather than linger on the sadness of Janis's untimely death, I want to celebrate her life with the following scenes:

Her kick-ass rendition of "Ball and Chain" at the Monterey Pop Festival in 1967, captured on film in the documentary "Monterey Pop." Besides Janis's astonishing performance, there's also the pleasure of watching the faces of members of the audience as the camera pans over them afterwards—one in particular, that of Mama Cass Elliott (no slouch in the singing department herself), who can be seen with a stunned expression on her face, clearly saying, "Wow!"

On "The Dick Cavett Show," the famous interview in which, amid telling the host that she would soon be attending her tenth annual high school reunion, Janis uttered the line I quoted earlier: "They laughed me out of class, out of town, and out of the state, man." To which she added, with bravado, accompanied by that wonderful cackle of hers, "So I'm going home."

(On YouTube now, there's footage of Janis at her high school reunion. Wearing rose colored glasses and a profusion of feathers in her hair while her former classmates look on, seemingly embalmed, Janis is full of herself, but the pain she obviously still feels is right there, threatening to break through the surface at any moment.)

This last scene happened much closer to home. As I've mentioned, I didn't have much in the way of friends in high school—and Daddy was always at work at the print shop, Mama was busy with her charges, my oldest sister was already away at college, and my second oldest sister was going through a period of hating me. But I did have that one aforementioned ally in Adeline McKenzie.

I adored Adeline, not only because she loved me back, but also for the simple reason that she was a lot of fun. Somewhere in her sixties by this time, I had known her since I was an infant, when she babysat my sisters and me, and gave me baths in the kitchen sink—or so I was told. She had the goods on my family, too—a matriarchy dominated by my haughty, evil maternal grandmother. More and more it was to her that I turned for attention, comfort and support. Simply being in the same room with her alone was reassuring because I felt that she understood me, and also that she empathized with me. But I always wanted more, and so one day I decided to do something that I had wanted to do for quite some time: I would play a song by Janis Joplin for her. But I was afraid: what if Adeline disliked Janis? Dismissed her? Or worst of all, what if she laughed and made fun of her—as so many others had done? These were my thoughts once again as I sat with Adeline one afternoon while she was ironing.

She hummed as she worked, steam rising from the iron, sweat streaming down her face, the words a listener could just make out always some variation of "Do Jesus," over and again. But what Adeline hummed was never true to the three short beats of that phrase, Do Je-sus. Instead she strung the syllables out, lengthening the vowels and entering the consonants, filling the words with air, and with life-experience, as if she was singing a dirge. Over and over, into verses and stanzas and refrains, so that by the time she paused (only to start all over again), Adeline had sung an entire song.

I reached for the album Cheap Thrills, then set the needle on the third track, George Gershwin's classic, "Summertime," just as I had imagined myself doing countless times. I said nothing to Adeline, who continued ironing and humming. I guessed that she probably knew the song itself but doubted she had heard Janis's version. Now I sat on my bed and watched Adeline's face as the slow and melancholy guitar intro segued into Janis wailing,

> *Summertime,*
> *Child, the living's easy....*

As Janis felt her way through the song, Adeline continued ironing, but I noticed that she had stopped her incessant humming, and also I thought that I noticed a very slight dip and sway added to her movements as she guided the iron back and forth across one of Daddy's few dress shirts.

When the song came to an end, I slowly got up off the bed, quietly lifted the needle from the record and removed it from the turntable. I put off looking at Adeline for as long as I could possibly stand it, I was so nervous; and when I did glance her way she just smiled at me, but said nothing. I remained silent, too, and yet I felt encouraged by her smile. A lifetime seemed to pass. I turned off the stereo, Adeline set down the iron, looked at me and said, "Robin, that girl can surely sing!" And my heart swelled! Janis's specific, expressed pain, in some ways the pain of all women (and some men), had merged with Adeline's own pain—that of a black woman, child of slaves—and with my own particular brand of misery, which I knew even then was secondary to Adeline's. It was a surprising, flowing, convergence, a kind of synthesis of the times that was so beautiful, yet so brief and ephemeral, I could have just cried: I got exactly what I wanted from the experience, and how often can anyone say that?

In the future there would be many more women singers for whom I would carry a torch—Billie Holiday, Nina Simone, Laura Nyro, Joni Mitchell, Edith Piaf, Patsy Cline, Karen Dalton, Patti Smith, Marianne Faithfull, and Amy Winehouse, to name a few. All of them have helped me survive, but Janis was the first, and the one who, as she said of Besse Smith, "showed me the air and taught me how to fill it."

garages

lung-gunned to hairline your neck the neck chain re-chained thigh
   thin off rubber, weight bench off hair-backed knuckle the voice I
   could trust trespassing for
if you kiss come choke where I drive from.

cursor back hogtie in jeans if you kiss the asking naked of back.
jaw. razor. thigh. trace a wet line and clamp

                    slick bitch on the calendar a motorcycle
                    cacti to her waist a rope cinched leather.
                    joelle. pulled how I want

mine pulled the few hairs feel around distraction: an oily office,
   machines pick up whole other machines the electric chests on
   wheels rags of gunk yellow beams ceiling

the industrial light, bad coffee fingernails the creamer dehydrated
   old meat shroud the collective nicotine angling barbwire out of
   grounds.

perimeter

                    wired headboard foot white turn-on you
                    smell on me different

          mark only I come to expect stock call me boy. backstairs get
          me down faster, thinking of the right geological term my
          hand a dip depression the rain and how the lobby floods I
          hate socks how they're tied to shoes.

    steel-toe dreamed
spokes from a motorbike to me finally the brunette just enough of
    an ottoman what

might be a problem my consumption how far my little speakeasies go
taking ten navy coverall asses spit over eel-tired bathing props in milk.

Water & Blood

Bettie, your stockings are too tight. They're squeezing the fat right out of you, & it's oiling your hair. Jesus is talking to you, B, Jesus is telling you your hair is too dark for clothes this small.

Have you seen my Suicide Girls? They have fish & Japanese blossoms lining rib bones. They leather & unleather, cut their bangs in all the right ways. Have you ever heard of bloodline tattoos? This blushing is for you.

There are no beaches in Tennessee. There are these willows, they fasten to wrists, pattern skin with feather-veins. They hold you there, topless, waiting for me or an arrest.

Bettie, can you Wonderwoman, Madonna, Uma or Demi for me? Can you disappear, slowly, forget your name, forget to unblur your face, forget to turn your bondagee around?

Everyone is schizophrenic. Everyone's a pinup.

These tattoos are inkless, all marks come from you. Take that ribbon from your hair, tie it around your throat.

O's and A's

Elise says I've been looking *phenomenal* lately, and her Os and As drop into me with all the extra affect of the real. "You're glowing," she says. It's true that I declared this the summer of high heels, and even in fall I'm still wearing my only pair. But I don't blush because my thighs are now kaleidoscopically elongated, because my Daisy Duke cut-offs crop a little of my cheeks, or 'cause I'm Betty Boop belted at the waist. I blush because this morning I called my boyfriend my boyfriend for the first time, right after I flipped this boyfriend on his belly, backed his ass into my face, rimmed him with the effort of my entire body and have never felt so butch.

Cheetahs

Lan and I are defining "ideological assault" at Cheetahs on Hollywood. A strip club where club means joint. "She has a real woman's body," I say. I think her name is Cherry. I regret the recourse to reality, but Lan agrees. Cherry's ass faces me from feet away. I am mesmerized. It's a cell in the process of mitosis, which is to say, it seems the source of life. Eve approaches. "Are you having fun?" she asks. "Are *you*?" Lan asks back. You can't touch the ladies even with the thrust stage—their aura is a proscenium not to be crossed. She asks if I'd like a dance. The dances are the money-makers not the tits. I put my arm around Lan, say "sorry, don't think she'd let me." She presses, "we get a lot like you in here, you can both come." "Thank you," I say, "but I don't think I'd let her." "Stay together," she says and walks off, while we wonder about the whiteness of my lie.

ELISE D'HAENE

Sometimes Slowly

WALK TOWARD THE BACK of the basement, decaf coffee in hand, just as the meeting starts and head toward my usual seat. There's a line of rectangular folding tables against the wall and on one of them, a 20ish-looking, tatted-up baby dyke sits picking at her fingernails, her legs dangle and swing as if she's in high school detention. As I approach, I can see there isn't enough space between the back row and the table she is on for me to get by easily unless she stops swinging so I can pass. I wish there was some kind of trap door in the floor. It's because I heard that song at Starbuck's.

I pause, clear my throat quietly. Ever so slowly, with a snarky expression fixed on her face, she holds her legs in the backswing position, and I scoot past.

Dee-Wee Debbie is already reading A.A.'s promises. *If we are painstaking about this phase of our development,* she says, *we will be amazed before we are half way through.*

The song was "Calling All Angels," a misery-soaked, funereal classic moaning through the speakers as I waited for my Decaf Venti.

As I take my seat on the one metal chair left with a cushion on it, Dee-Wee Debbie continues with The Promises: *We are going to know a new freedom and a new happiness.*

She's called Dee-Wee because she has had seven Driving While

Intoxicated arrests, served a short stint in prison, and racked up over
$50,000 worth of fines and attorney fees.

The song sent me tripping over loose floorboards in my mind—
one careless step can pitch me into the catacombs of drunk nights,
putting dead men's ashes on my tongue, chasing them down with
tequila shots, and retching at having to sing that song one more god-
damned time at one more goddamned memorial service. Armando
and I had our own version: *Fucking all angels, fucking all angels, fuck
me through this world, don't fuck me alone.*

I glance to the front of the room at Martha, my sponsor who chairs
the meeting. She's a pudgy die-hard Catholic, with a head of tight
grey curls. Sad, puffy prunes seem to hang under her eyes. She attends
one meeting a day ever since she stopped drinking over 45 years ago.

Martha is old-school A.A., a Big Book thumper, who calls bars
"gin joints" and says things like "God told me to put the cork in
the jug or die." She treats me like a beginner, even though I've been
sober ten years. She says, "Pie-face, every morning we wake up, we're
beginners."

Martha nods vigorously, mouthing the promises as Debbie delivers
them: *We will not regret the past nor wish to shut the door on it.*

Martha understands that there are days when my entire structure
collapses and I fall into the past. It happens to her too, she says, but
she just calls it "stinkin' thinkin'."

When I fall, I sometimes feel something falling along with me.
It's a physical sensation, not just emotional, an awareness of myself
descending through space and it's as though I have a companion
falling with me—a falling buddy—and together, colliding, electrons
merging, I understand that my falling friend is really all of my dead
queer brothers fused into one being, making my descent less terrify-
ing, then slowly they melt away, dissolve, leaving an emptiness in the
space inside and around me that they had just occupied.

The clank of metal slaps me back to the room. Six empty chairs
away from me, Baby Dyke has plopped herself down. Her left knee

jitters like a boy's. She has a slash of magenta hair, wears a sheen of sweat along with ripped jeans and a sleeveless t-shirt. From where I sit, her arms are so tattooed they seem bruised or stained. Even as I turn away, her twitchy electricity causes my chest to tighten with anxiety-by-association. *Fear of people and of economic insecurity will leave us*, Debbie says, though I'm a stellar example of that particular promise not coming through.

I never got a DUI. I hit a tree once driving down a curvy road in Topanga Canyon going about 5 miles per hour. When I got out to inspect the damage, I thought I heard the tree moan, so I threw my arms around it like the sloppy, maudlin drunk that I was and wept. The memory still makes me cringe.

No matter how far down the scale we have gone, we will see how our experience can benefit others.

The basement we're in has cheap, 1950's wood paneling on the walls, tiled flooring that looks clinically depressed and urine-colored fluorescent lighting.

Our whole attitude and outlook upon life will change.

I focus on my cup of decaf coffee, lift it to my lips, and take a long sip that contains a mouthful of coffee grounds. Some scratch at my throat as they go down, and others—tiny bitter balls—stick to my tongue.

Are these extravagant promises? Debbie asks.

*We **think not**,* the members of the meeting answer back, though I miss the moment, distracted by the girl, and my tongue as it plays hide and seek with the stray grounds of coffee in my mouth.

They are being fulfilled among us—sometimes quickly, sometimes slowly. They will always materialize if we work for them.

I BEND TO RETRIEVE a dollar from my backpack so I'm ready when the collection basket is passed. I steal a look at the girl's arm, wanting to know what her tattoos reveal. Now, she's four seats away from me. (Did I count wrong the first time?) As I pretend to rummage in my bag, I see that she is picking and digging at a scab on her arm, causing bits of crusty skin and blood to ooze under her short, bitten-to-the-nubs nail. There are several scabs in various stages of woundedness, some fresh and weepy, others scarred over. I read about this new trend in self-mutilation. They're called Scabbers—drilling into their flesh with their nails; some go so deep they hit bone.

I grab my water bottle, take a long gulp, wash away the coffee grounds, and focus my attention to the front, where today's speaker, Coma Kat, is at the podium. As implied by her A.A. nickname, Kat has been in three comas due to alcohol.

"God was there, man," Kat says, "because my fucking cellphone, which I thought I fucking lost, was on the floor behind the toilet. Don't ask me how it got there. When I fell out of the shower, I broke my ankle. My foot sorta hung at the end of my leg like a dead fish. But I was gone. I didn't feel shit."

Martha tenses up, runs a quick finger under her nose each time Debbie says "fucking" or "shit." She is one hundred percent against swearing in meetings.

Martha had parked her Buick Riviera in the alley behind a gin joint that opened at 9 a.m., trying to make sure that no one in town would know she was inside (though everybody did). Sitting at the bar on her morning stool, Martha put together enough "just one more" and "Hank, give me another" so that the temperature outside went from the high 60s to the low 80s. Even though the driver's side window was opened a few inches, her Labrador, Rufus, died of heatstroke on the floor in the backseat of the car, where he was found, his large body curled up as tight as possible in the last square of shade he could find. She didn't know this until she got home, doesn't remember driving back to her house. She was whipping up a quick meatloaf, peeling potatoes for some mashed, and she called out for Rufus to come get a bit of raw ground beef she'd set aside for him. Rufus didn't come.

The room always takes on an extra layer of stillness when Martha tells that part of her story. It's a silence so heavy that I can almost feel all the metal chairs holding all of our bodies sink a few inches into the floor and then into the earth from the weight of Martha's admission. She'll bite her bottom lip a few times as she recounts her story, and rub her palms hard on her cheeks like she's scrubbing a skillet encrusted with days-old dried egg.

All at once, Baby Dyke shimmies into the seat next to mine, startling me, and whispers, "hey," then stretches her legs out. I sort of nod back, look down, and see, through the rip in her jeans, that she has tight, thick quads, like people who ride bikes or go Spinning. Like Mel, my best friend a thousand years ago, whose quad muscles visibly contracted beneath her 501's when she breathed.

I slightly turn my body away, hoping to dissuade Baby Dyke from deciding to sit on my lap. I remember the night Mel and I decided to have sex with each other because we were both single, it was 105 degrees outside with Santa Ana winds igniting brush fires all around, and because we both truly believed that the world was hurtling toward its end. When she straddled me, she squeezed those quads tight, trapping me in her grip so I could not move, then jammed her wet cunt against mine, while her sweet fingers tortured my nipples. We were both stripped naked, the smell of sticky sex-sweat leaking from every pore. For a moment I saw Mel as a boa constrictor and her cunt a gaping jaw, and ever so slowly she was going to suck my whole body inside of her, consume me bit by bit.

Afterward, we sat in the bathtub filled with cool water, and she started reading an article by the gay writer and activist Larry Kramer, who wrote that we were all going to go insane living this epidemic every minute of every day while the rest of the world goes on as if nothing is happening, and I grabbed the magazine and flung it out the bathroom door, because I didn't want to hear what I already knew was true—we were either dying or going stark raving mad.

"What's so fucked up," Kat says, her voice pulling me back into the room, "is that people are always asking me what it was like to be in a coma—*fucking* boneheads. I don't *fucking* remember. I was in a *fucking* coma!" Ripples of laughter fill the room punctuated by the loud crackle of my plastic bottle—now gripped in my fist. I bend down, pretend to rummage in my backpack for something, then stuff the bottle into it. I glance up at Martha, who is rubbing and rubbing her face due to all the "fucking" talk.

Mel moved back home to St. Paul, hooked up with her ex-girl-friend, said she was tired of burying friends. We stopped calling each other. But I don't remember why. Was it my drinking? Did I drunk-dial Mel one too many times in a blackout? Maybe she changed her number. I want to make amends to her, but Martha says I've tried long enough to track her down, and that I need to "let go, let God."

I do remember one phone call. It was after midnight, L.A. time. I was blotto, but not in a blackout. Mel answered in faraway voice, not distant geographically, but long gone from the landscape of emotion we once crawled together. I didn't even say hello, I was pissed at her for leaving me. I just started slurring names into the phone from a sheet of paper, a list that we had started together: "James, Gary, Barry, Steve, Eugene, Adam, Rick, Ara, Michael, Christopher, Tovar, Gil, Schlomo, Rodney, Armando…Armando…Armando. . . ."

I remember hearing Mel breathe. I remember wanting to crawl inside Mel's mouth. I don't remember what else might have been said or not said. I woke up clutching the paper, my body half on, half off the couch, the phone emitting that cursed, whiny beep.

Armando.

In the final stages of his disease, he would gaze up at me as if he were my baby—make cooing sounds, smile crookedly, and grasp at my nose, lips, ears, and breasts and he'd giggle and I'd giggle too and make my best mommy noises back, stretching the flesh on my face into silly expressions. Maybe his eyes had gone too, the way of his atrophied brain and all he could see was a blur of color and motion—but I saw him seeing something that I couldn't see, which made him coo for hours on end—new galaxies being born, or maybe some kind of vision reserved for the dying. Eventually, I would push his morphine button releasing more of the liquid lullaby into his veins so I could go outside and sit alone and smoke and drink, summoning up the most thunderous imaginary arguments with Armando's real mother and father, who were not there, would not come.

Mel left just before Armando died.

A hand touches my shoulder, yanks me from my reverie. Baby Dyke holds out the donation basket. I drop in my dollar. "Thanks," I say, not realizing that Kat has finished speaking and several arms are up from members wanting to share.

I see that tattooed on the girl's right hand—the three middle fingers—are the letters O-U-T, and on her left hand, thumb to pinkie, is P-R-O-U-D. My clit releases a slight pulse and I want to give my groin a time-out for misbehavior. I'm old enough to be this girl's mother.

I wonder what it would be like to get fucked by a fist with PROUD written on it. My cunt aches. I'm afraid it will moan like the tree I hit.

I'VE COME TO BELIEVE that I'm living whole other lives, layers of them stacked on top of one another, all happening at the same time, and in one of them I've been housed permanently on a psychiatric ward. In the ward are dozens, no, hundreds, maybe thousands of us, and we are suffering from a malady called Queer Survival Syndrome. It's very much like the ailment once called Soldier's Heart then Shell Shock and now Post-Traumatic Stress Disorder. There, I am Sanitarium Kelly, and I wear paper slippers and the only thing I look forward to each day is the tiny paper cups of tablets I am given. Once in awhile we are allowed to have a talent night or pizza and caffeine-free soda is brought in, but none of us are capable of letting our queer flags fly. We don't ACT UP one bit. In fact, you wouldn't know unless you were told that all of us had once been very queer and very gay.

When I told Martha about my stacked life theory she rubbed her face for a while then said: "If you turn it over and don't let go of it, you will be upside down."

"My name is Walter and I like to say that I have a *devastating*, *incurable*, and *lethal* disease called alcoholism and the only medicine offered is a chair at an A.A. meeting on a daily basis." His nasally, kazoo-like voice immediately makes my lips droop.

"Hi, Walter," the members respond limply.

A tiny grunt escapes from my mouth. Baby Dyke giggles in response, elbows me. Our eyes meet and we both smile. Walter is a whiner and listening to him makes me want to drink. As he has at this meeting for the last two months, he goes on and on about his *miserable* experience with his *horrifying* new neighbors who have four *repulsive* yapping Pekinese.

Martha interrupts him: "Let's keep our shares focused on our problems as they relate to our alcoholism."

Walter snorts: "I am a dipsomaniac! Every moment of every day is related to this terminal illness!"

Baby Dyke knocks her knee against mine. We both strain to keep from laughing. When I was her age, I forced myself to go to a lesbian support group in order to test the waters of my wobbly sexual identity. I stayed for a whole five minutes. It was because of the boy, just barely a toddler. One of his mommy's was holding him, explaining to other group members that she and her S.O. had used a sperm donor and turkey baster and her S.O. gave birth and both of them were extremely disappointed that *he* wasn't a *she*. "It is what it is," she sighed, harshly pushing a pacifier into the boy's mouth when he began to make a tender *whah whah* sound, legs flapping, as he pointed at a sliver of sunlight dancing on the wall.

Since I was not interested on that particular day in being arrested for use of force in the act of kidnapping a child, I bolted from the room, hit Santa Monica Boulevard and ran to see Armando at Ripples, a gay men's bar—men who were once little boys with mothers who were elated the moment their slippery, penis-wagging infant was hung upside down and slapped on the ass by a male doctor, and then, years later, those very same mothers rejected their boys-turned-gay because they developed a desire to have their asses slapped by men.

Armando made me a Margarita, said he was hoping I'd get laid after the support group, though I told him it didn't work that way with women. He loved to give me advise on being a woman. He'd ply me with his leftover cosmetic samples that he got for his drag show and several times insisted on doing my makeup before I went out, though I always ended up looking like a cross between Lily Munster and Barbara Bush.

This was B.D. (Before Death). Before Armando and his sequins and pink feather boa and painted face and lean, brown legs, before— poof—Armando and all that glitter died. Then Armando's new boyfriend committed suicide just after Armando's funeral because he had it too and saw how the disease peeled away all the beauty from his beloved "Sue Veneer"—Armando's drag name—which is all I have left of him—souvenir cosmetics held in a box along with photos, birthday cards, twizzle sticks, Ripples matchbooks, cocktail umbrellas, and a prayer card from his funeral.

I could never have tattooed OUT PROUD onto my fists back then. As I was learning how to slide my hand inside women's cunts and resting my opened wet mouth onto the opened wet mouth of a lover, a sniper was killing my brothers, one by one. We snorted poppers on dance floors, wept and wept, and drank ourselves into oblivion as the bodies piled up.

In one of my other stacked lives that I haven't told Martha about, I'm Fairfax Kelly, a homeless, toothless woman who parks my soiled shopping bags at Fairfax and Santa Monica Boulevard, just a few blocks from where this meeting is. I smell like a mix of sour gym socks and bottom-shelf Gordon's vodka, and have bloated ankles and feet that are pocked with open wounds. I wear men's extra large flip-flops, and a grimy, threadbare housecoat. There's a Whole Foods on my corner and at 10:30 each night, I wobble to the back of the store to the loading dock where there are shelves of spoilage and I have myself a feast.

Some of the baby fags and dykes stop and ask me how I'm doing. They're fresh and clean—wear Fred Segal outfits, plan weddings, register at Williams-Sonoma, and adopt third-world babies. I tell them about when I was their age, how we took to the streets, back when we were still queer and angry. And we'd block Santa Monica Boulevard, stop traffic, push our bodies against gun-toting cops who wore yellow gloves and hospital masks, and we'd chant at those panty-wipe assholes: *Your gloves don't match your shoes!! Your gloves don't match your shoes!!*

I told Martha last week that sometimes I have to pretend to be someone else just to get through the day, just to walk down the sidewalk from my apartment to the grocery store, or to stay seated in my chair at my cubicle where I enter data from medical records into a computer. Lately, I've been pretending to be Maria Sharapova, and I'll stand erect, walk with confidence, my shoulders thrust back, chest forward: I am the number one fucking tennis player in all the world! I screech and howl every time I hit the ball, so fuck off! (I didn't say the fuck part to Martha).

"You know what I think, Martha," I said, "everyone crushed under the thumb of sorrow should be allowed to screech and howl as much as they want."

She nodded and made affirming sounds, then said, "Pie-face," taking my hands in hers, "the road to sobriety is a simple journey for confused people with a complicated disease," she then paused and asked, "Is Maria Sharapova sober?"

I don't know why, but when Martha says simple shit like that, it helps.

I close my eyes, lean up against my wounded friend. Maybe, she's an angel, and the wretchedness of the world is howling from each scab. Maybe in another life, stacked between Sanitarium Kelly and Fairfax Kelly, is Sylvia Plath Kelly, and she and I are young lovers. We write awful poetry, drink too much, and fuck each other with proud fists.

But in this life, here in this basement, Baby Dyke nudges me with her arm of scabs, hands me a torn piece of paper on which she's scribbled her name, "Frankie," then gives it to me with her chewed up pen. I write my name down *and* my phone number, hand it back, obeying Martha's mantra in my head: *Our primary purpose is to stay sober and to help other alcoholics to achieve sobriety.*

Frankie's hand tremors slightly as she writes on the other side of the paper, then rolls it up into a tight ball and presses it into my hand.

I unravel the slip, stare at the question.

Will you be my sponsor?

A panicky heat sparks from Frankie's body.

Inside I can feel a drill grinding into the gut-depth of me. Falling, rising, dropping, lifting, digging and digging until a hot, molten yes gushes from my core.

"Yes," I say, meeting Frankie's eyes.

Martha's voice pulls our attention back to the meeting. "Let's have a moment of silence for the still sick and suffering in and outside of these rooms."

We bow our heads. I reach for Frankie's hand.

BRENT ARMENDINGER

Casual Sex

You're not to whom it may concern
but whom could make an opening in him
like the smoke in this language
I intrude upon while he, blubbering
of heart, was all too tucked
inside the minus signs
I strung around my neck
until I could no longer
hold my head up to look at you,
the blackout in me jingling.

He of dog leash, of muzzle,
climbing in reverse, a thief
through my cartoon window.
I found him like I find everything –
on my way home from the euphemism
on the wrong side of town,
the mouth inside of brick
where night can go on being night
until it finally falls asleep
inside some other animal's ambition.

That's where I buried the clocks,
in case you're wondering, the coils
inside them stammered. The nightingales
are busy inventing a suitable anthem for my face
as I wipe it clean of every him
inside that oubliette. And how easy
it is to fall inside of falling,
my spit inside of him

inside of him makes me you,
a double preposition, a corridor
in briefly and stumble into birdcall,
the mind outside the mind in me.

ZOE DONALDSON

my erotic double

is a plain little boy. i dip in to
write it all down, smooth
misunderstandings from his
face, but he cries and tugs until
he leaves to horse around with
the others. it is just a tuesday.
we meet in the park for double
dates. boys buck and howl and
smash and then it is time to
picnic. watch: he pounds the
ground, fills fists with wads of
grass, stomps feet until soil
churns to pulp, spits pennies
into unsuspecting mouths. other
mothers don't appear to have
this problem. i snatch at his
scrunched face, pluck fuzz from
his peach body. it is time for a
bite: he refuses my arms, full of
bright, wet oranges. he won't
let me dress any of his wounds.
blood is the only sport. he
stands tall, a thin body struck by
lightning. proud boy, using new
words every day. back arched,
his puffer-fish belly, smooth of
spikes, puts space between us.
we both glare at the loud

handprint left on my breast,
heaving hollow of his chest. but
when he rests, when the sun
finally passes over the swings,
we both find peace. it is time for
sleep: a sleep for the boy giant
with fitful fever dreams. the
four corners of our blanket are
stretched. the body is scaffold
and he scales it—hands in my
hair, mouth barely meets my
breast, small feet brush against
my shins. i trace the tiniest river
of wet down his heart-shaped
back at full beat. it is time for a
mistake: he slips in to still
himself. i try to reach down and
help him, whisper new words
like *consummate* and *cumulus* into
the coil of his ear, rub one out,
but he grows heavy every day
the growing boy he is my baby
boy.

SAM ROSS

Demi-god Ready to Abduct Extremely Willing Shepherd

You tend sheep with your sheep dog.
        I am only one thing all the time:

                I want, I want, I want. There is nothing else.
        Mostly, I tend to go older,

but I like how you play with the sheep dog,
        indifferent to the sheep.

                It is *the* unknowable mystery to me, not these
        Arcadian duties—desire. Myself,

I've been taken in a field only once or twice.
        At Jewish summer camp, humid air

                hung with enough hormones to kindle
        an orgy if anyone had thought to,

and all the boys ran wild together
        naked through the blue night.

                I mean to say I do not believe the acolyte-act.
        As much as mine, it is your move

when one sweltering afternoon I fly down
        through the canyon, from leaning clouds.

WAYNE JOHNS

Where Your Children Are (1981)

THAT SUMMER A WOMAN'S voice interrupted TV shows every hour to announce the time and ask, *Do you know where your children are?*

A city-wide curfew was in effect: no one under eighteen allowed out after sundown. But that didn't stop us from sliding out my bedroom window and easing into the backyard, as into dark water. I had stashed, in my back pocket, the allowance I'd been saving since I found out my best friend Trace was coming to stay with us for a week. An orange-tinged moon was snared in the pines. The crickets' pulsing stopped as we approached. Fireflies still signaled through the branches of the water oak—its leaves dog-eared and riddled with holes from the profusion of tent caterpillars. Earlier that summer Mother had given me and Trace some of those long fireplace matches and told us to burn as many webs as we could reach. We climbed up and torched their nests spun in the forks of branches. I recoiled as they sizzled and melted, then we watched as the caterpillars dropped to the ground, still writhing. The smell of singed hair made me choke.

WHENEVER THE WOMAN'S voice asked its perfunctory and vaguely threatening question, Mother would answer, "Good Lord, I just hope it doesn't turn out to be a white man murdering all those black children." I guess she figured if the killer was white, someone would start killing white kids for revenge.

"Must be a Homo doing it," my father would add, peering over *The Atlanta Constitution*. "Why else would only boys' bodies keep turning up in the river?" He looked at me over the top of his black-rimmed reading glasses, "Tell me that."

I shrugged and cringed, getting up to go to my room.

H E WAS TALKING about the Chattahooochee river, which cuts the northwest section of the city, not far from where we lived. Trace's mother was leaving town and he was going to stay with us the week before school started. He had slept over before, but never stayed a whole week. I could hardly sleep at night, thinking of him lying beside me. Before he got there, Mother said, "Lord knows, with all this craziness, his mother feels better with him staying in *this* neighborhood." By that, of course, she meant a white neighborhood. When she spoke like this, I bit down on my tongue and the back of my neck tingled, as if a caterpillar was crawling up it. I prayed she wouldn't say anything like that in front of Trace.

His real name was Tracy, but he hated it because he said that was a girl's name. Since it was August, the Allegheny Chinkapins were in bloom. I didn't know them by name then, only by the bleachy scent of their flowers.

"You smell the cum trees?" I asked, because I'd heard my cousin say that.

"What do you know about it? I bet you don't even skeet yet, huh?"

"What?"

"Maybe I'll show you later," Trace laughed. "How far's Michelle's house from here?"

"Pretty far."

"How far?"

"A mile… maybe two."

"I bet no black families live around here, do they?" He spit.

"I don't know," I lied, "I think so."

"Yeah right, Kevin. You would know." Then after a moment, "Come on, let's walk to Michelle's house."

"We shouldn't go far. There's still a curfew," I protested.

"Don't be such a wussy. Besides, what're you worried about? They haven't found any dead white boys floating down the Hooch," he pushed me.

I didn't care for peeping through windows, but liked any excuse to be that close, wedged against him, feeling a surge when our arms brushed. Crouched beneath a lit window, peering over the sill through a slit in the curtains, we were lucky enough to see her undressing. Trace adjusted himself, even slipped a hand inside his sweat pants. I watched out of the corner of my eye, pretending to be excited by the small pink buds on her chest, the triangle of new hair between her legs, when I was really only thrilled by this secret between us.

The porch light came on. We dropped flat on the grass and I couldn't stop trembling, my heart stuttering against the ground. Clutched in the same position we fell in, arms tangled, his fingernails digging into my arm and shoulder, faces so close I could feel his breath on my cheek. It smelled like warmed milk. The front door opened.

"Who's there?" Michelle's mother rasped. We stayed still, gripping each other tighter.

The porch light went off. I didn't have facial hair yet and Trace only had a few wisps of fine hairs above his lip, so there was no grating when our cheeks touched. Only softness and heat.

Trace pulled away, leaving my cheek tingling as if I'd just been slapped. He looked around, but didn't get up. I couldn't see Michelle's mother, but knew she was still there since the door hadn't closed.

A strip of light sliced across the yard from the window of Michelle's bathroom. In my head I kept repeating, *Just pretend I'm Michelle, Just pretend I'm Michelle*, as if casting a spell. I couldn't see his face. I had never kissed anyone before. Well, not counting the time I had pecked Michelle at school behind the backstop. I didn't really want to, had only done it to make Trace jealous. His face suddenly closer. I convinced myself some force was pulling us together, like magnets.

I was about to ask if Michelle's mother was still there when I grazed the velvet of his lips. So we were practically kissing. I was afraid to move, afraid of undoing the moment we were wrapped up in like strangers. Then the screen door slammed, the front door closed, and the lock clicked. Trace got up and ran, leaving me in the dark yard. I hesitated, rubbing the sickles his fingernails had dug into my shoulder, before running after him.

Down the road, he was throwing rocks at a street lamp, alive with insects, while bats dove into the light. In Biology we had learned they don't really see the light; the movement of the insects draws them to it. I walked slowly toward Trace. Neither of us spoke. We took turns trying to burst the bulb. When we noticed the bats going for the rocks, we threw a little lower each time to see the quick flicker of them come tumbling down like pieces of the night sky thrown back at us.

Once the bats got bored and stopped diving, Trace said, "Race you to the end of the block."

He won, as usual. Then we started walking to the Quickie Mart, which was open all night. Trace kept running a palm over his close cut hair as if brushing it. He had been trying to get waves because the guy Michelle was going steady with, Dexter, had them—perfectly spaced ripples running through his hair. Trace used to say he hoped D. lost his waves. I guess he figured that would also mean he'd lose Michelle. At the beginning of that summer my hair was still in wings but I had gotten a fade before Trace came to stay with us. I felt like someone else because he said it was 'dope'.

"How much you want to bet Michelle drops D. as soon as school starts," Trace slid his palm over his scalp.

"Keep wishing," I said, trying to discourage him.

"Please, he's not *even* light-skinned enough to be going with a white girl once we start high school."

"Says who?"

"My cousin said…"

"Your big-mouth cousin already graduated."

T HE HIGH SCHOOL we were about to start was called Crossed Keys—supposedly because the area was once an Indian trading post—the point where four trails converged. There was a neighborhood behind the school known as "Indian Village" because all the streets had names like Coosawatee and Okachobee; of course no Native Americans, that I knew of, had ever lived in those rows of what Mother called 'shotgun' houses. This was still years before the Brookhaven MARTA station opened, before the little houses started to get bought up and torn down and replaced by those towering monstrosities, that seem to spring up in weeks, with three or four floors and no yard because the house itself takes up the whole lot. But some of the people refused to sell. To this day, you can drive through what was known as Indian Village and see one shotgun, with a rusted truck parked in front of the overgrown yard, flanked on either side by two of the new models, one of which seems to be made almost entirely of glass. The man who owns the dilapidated shotgun is known as Gus, and he swears he'll die in the house he was born in. Because my father also grew up in this neighborhood, he had hired Gus one time to put new shingles on our house. I remember my father going out to talk to him and coming back inside to get his wallet.

When my mother asked what was the matter he said, "I've got to run to the store."

"Um-um-um…" shaking her head, "What did I tell you? A leopard can't change its spots."

"Don't start, Mother."

"It is a little early in the day to get started drinking isn't it?"

After he slammed the front door, I went to sit beside her on the bed while she sniffed and peered through the blinds. I wanted to know where Dad had gone and when he was coming back. When she said he went to get the men something to drink, I must've said I wanted to go make them Lemonade, or something, because she said: "They're not really thirsty, honey. Now go on and get out from up under me."

She went into the bathroom to splash water on her face and look in the mirror. "I told your daddy not to get tangled back up with that bunch of rednecks." I wanted to ask what that meant, but I peered through the blinds to try and see them.

"Their necks don't look red," I said, forever the literalist.

"Buster, and I'm telling you this for your own good, you'd better not mess with me right now."

"I'll be quiet… I promise."

"Get out from up under me so I can breathe," she said coming towards me. I ran for the door then. "And close that door so I can pull myself together," she yelled.

I tried to imagine her in pieces, like a jigsaw, but could only picture her face on the cartoon man in that game called Operation; the nose lighting red and buzzing if the mini tweezers touched the sides as you tried to be the first to remove all the bad or broken parts. I equated the sound of the buzzer with pain, and the man's face on the game perpetually grimaced. My hand never steady enough.

MOTHER DROVE ME down one of the dead-end streets in Indian Village once to show me the house my father had grown up in. I was in the backseat on top of the stacks of *The Atlanta Journal* she delivered each morning. It was that silvery hour of dawn before the sun actually rises, so I was still half asleep as I looked out the window, and I didn't know how I was supposed to feel about the house. No matter how many times I tried, I was never able to find it again. All the houses on the street looked alike then anyway; and I'm sure it's long gone by now. I mainly recall that green vines had claimed the shed on the side of the house, and the door to the shed was missing. I wouldn't have known to call the vine kudzu or that it was a parasite which, given enough time, could strip the bark and branches from, even kill, a full-grown pine.

"There were twelve of them in that little piss-ant house." She shook her head and seemed upset. "I'll never understand people that can treat a child any such as that, much less their own."

"Who lives here Mommy?"

"White Trash. What else can you call it?"

"What's that?"

"Take a good look, son." I stared at the black space inside the shed. I knew something terrible must be hiding inside; I figured it was the white trash. "That right there is the reason me and your daddy drove to Tennessee and got married and moved out when we were sixteen years old. Yes sir, take a long hard look Buster and be thankful you have a mama and daddy that bust their asses seven days a week, so you can have better, and don't just lay around drunk and have babies they don't want and can't feed. Lord God, as long as I live I'll never understand why you would let innocent children…."

Then she was more just talking to herself, or praying, and crying some, and I knew not to ask anymore questions. As we were driving away, I turned to look back at the matchbox house. I felt something new then—a cross between shame and fear—though I didn't know exactly what I had to be ashamed or afraid of. I laid down on the stacks of newspapers. When I felt the bumps of the car going over the railroad tracks, Mother said aloud "That right there is what you call the *wrong* side of the tracks, son." I pretended to be asleep and she reached one hand back to touch my face, which was pressed against columns of words I couldn't read though I knew that, somehow, our lives depended on them. The moldy smell of the papers always clung to the seats, our clothes, even after they'd all been delivered.

T RACE AND I HAD HOPPED a freight train once and rode it all the way to his grandmother's house in Lynwood Park. The first time we drove to pick him up, my heart raced. I stared out the window. Sides of buildings and walls had been tagged with names in bright colors. I imagined us tagging our names, KEV 'N' TRACE, on the side of an overpass, in huge block letters.

As we passed the basketball court I pressed my nose to the passenger-side glass, gaping at the game of shirts versus skins. When we got to Trace's house, there was a touch football game going on in the street. I started to get out, but Trace came running up to the truck, waving either to the other kids or to his grandmother silhouetted in a window, keeping watch. Trace said because of all the missing children he hadn't been able to leave the street in front of his house all summer.

Dad's truck had a camper and we both rode in back. When we passed under streetlights, I stood out like a negative. I wanted to stay in Trace's neighborhood which looked so alive, unlike our neighborhood—locked in its perpetual silence except for the occasional yelping dog, or the moan of trains in the distant night.

T HERE WAS NO TRAIN COMING as we walked along the tracks to the Quickie Mart. You could always hear the ding of the crossing signal before you ever heard the whistle. The only sound was the crunch of our sneakers on the gravel between the crossties and, of course, frogs calling from the creek.

Back in fifth grade, everyone would ride their bikes along the tracks, until this kid, Jerry Elmire, got caught between the ties. I heard the train dragged him a hundred yards before grinding to a halt. After that, the railroad was off limits. The county fenced off the section that ran through our neighborhood, even topped the fence with coils of razor wire. But that didn't keep us out. There were places where the fence had been lifted or cut just enough to scoot under.

The tracks ran parallel to Peachtree Industrial, and both extended from the suburbs through the heart of downtown. At night the faint outlines of the buildings in the distance lit up like rockets. Like everything else that summer, they seemed filled with promise and threat.

The bell tower at Oglethorpe sounded the hour.

"It's eleven o'clock, do you know where your children are?" I said.

"Shut up! That shit's not funny," Trace pushed me. We cut through a thin strip of woods to get to the Quickie Mart. Trace stopped and I bumped into him.

"What?"

"I heard something," he said. We stood still. The leaves rustled. We ran the rest of the way, sticks and briars carving red traceries down our arms and legs.

The store was too bright. The bearded man behind the counter, black tee-shirt almost, but not quite, stretched over his gut, eyed us as we got Doritos and sodas. Next to the register, I picked up a tin of Skoal Bandits and set it on the counter. The man rang up the candy and sodas, but paused when he got to the dip.

"How old you boys?"

"Sixteen," I lied. I was twelve and Trace had just turned thirteen.

"A little late to be out and about, ain't it?"

"My dad sent us to get him some dip," I tried to lower my voice.

"Your Daddie dips Skoal Bandits?"

"He said he wanted to try it."

The man lifted a red plastic cup, spit into it, then tossed the dip in the bag. As the change funneled out of the register and into the circular tray, he said, "You boys better get on home. Specially you," he said, pointing at Trace. "If the cops catch you, they'll lock you up for breaking curfew." And then, under his breath, "And that ain't all you got to worry 'bout."

The bell that was tied to the door jangled. We walked fast to the edge of the parking lot, then broke into a sprint. We ran until we were out of sight of the store, then stopped, laughing and gasping.

I put the dip in my back pocket like I'd seen my older cousin do—a faded circle worn into his cut-off jeans. We didn't think about cutting through the woods to walk back along the tracks, we just walked along Peachtree, eating Doritos and washing them down with soda.

After we left the store that night, the man behind the counter might have called the police, or maybe an undercover officer was driving the beat-up white truck that slowed as it passed us. But we kept walking and the white truck went a little farther before we saw brake lights. No other cars were on the road. The buildings in the distance seemed a hundred miles away.

"It's backing up," Trace said and we ran behind the Animal Hospital. I could hear the motor growling. We waited until we couldn't hear it, then ran to the corner behind the abandoned gas station.

"Let's hide," I whispered. We crawled under a rusted tractor. Gravel dug into my back and my heart hammered harder than it had earlier in Michelle's front yard.

"Oh God," Trace whispered. In my head, convinced we were being punished, I asked forgiveness for kissing Trace: *If you let us get away...* I prayed silently. Then I thought, *Save Trace.* I pictured myself rolling out from under the tractor, and then my pale body floating in the muddy river, the killer's handprints bruised around my throat. Then my parents would be sorry for the terrible things they said, and Trace would be safe and know how much I loved him. But, of course, I didn't move.

The truck rolled by. I could hear my breathing and covered my mouth. The truck roared up to the railroad crossing and stopped, then backed up real slow. Headlights passed over the tractor as it pulled around to the front of the gas station. The truck door opened and slammed. Footsteps on concrete, then gravel. Trace grabbed my hand, which was on his shoulder. I held my breath. The footsteps stopped. In my head I kept pleading. I inhaled through my nose, afraid he'd hear me if I breathed through my mouth. Trace's fingernails were digging into my hand. That small pain seemed the only thing that kept me from moving or screaming. Cigarette smoke burned my nostrils. I saw the glowing cherry hit the ground and roll, suspended in the darkness. It stopped at eye level and seemed close enough to touch. Footsteps again—this time the gravel crunched, pause, then a louder crunch—that sounded like he was limping. One of my hands went numb. I squeezed my eyes shut and when I opened them again the red eye of the cigarette was still there, staring. I heard the truck door open and close, then the ignition, then gravel crunching, then screeching tires as the truck peeled back onto Peachtree.

We slid out and ran. That was the only time I was able to keep up with Trace. We passed the cemetery and Brookhaven Baptist church, then dove behind a row of shrubs at the corner of someone's yard. We waited to make sure the truck wasn't coming.

The moon had lost the mock orange it held when we first left my house—it had turned white and almost full, like an eyeball rolled into the socket. The sky was starless. Maybe the stars were just obscured by clouds, or invisible because of the glow of the city. As we lay there, panting, a few stars gradually became visible, and the outlines of pines, blacker than the sky.

After several minutes, I whispered "Do you think it's safe?"

WE AVOIDED THE STREET, cutting through back yards the rest of the way to my house. When we snuck back in my bedroom window and sat against the headboard looking at the small black and white television that had belonged to my grandmother, I still didn't feel safe. Before long, the soothing and disturbing woman's voice announced it was one o'clock in the morning, then asked: "Do you know where your children are?"

I fell asleep and woke up with Trace's leg thrown over me. I had a hard-on, but it hurt because it was pinned downward by his leg. I tried to lie perfectly still so the new feeling would last. I wanted to adjust myself, but that would have meant working my hand under his leg and possibly waking him. So I wavered between pain and ecstasy until I finally dozed off. When I woke, Trace had gotten up and gone to sleep on the sofa.

I WAS TOO TIRED TO GO outside the next day, and it was raining anyway. Neither of us mentioned what had happened. We spent the day watching Kung-Fu Theatre. Trace convinced me to call Michelle. I kept her on the phone as long as possible because he laid down beside me and pressed his ear to the receiver to hear her voice.

By evening the rain had stopped. My parents were in the living room watching *Wheel of Fortune*. As we walked through the kitchen, I put a finger to my lips to warn Trace to be quiet. I could hear the wheel ticking, slowing down. A man's voice asked, "Can I buy an 'I'?" Mother said "How dumb can you be?" There was a buzzer and then another man's voice said "Oh, I'm sorry, there's no 'I'."

As soon I opened the back door, Mother yelled "Kev-innn!"

"What?" I yelled.

"Don't 'what' me young man. Don't leave this yard, it's getting dark."

Everything was still damp, and the trees were dripping. The sun burned through the last clouds like the lit tip of a cigarette. I remembered the can of Skoal Bandits still in the back pocket of my jeans. I tucked one of the packets inside my bottom lip the way I'd seen my cousin do it, and Trace did the same. We jumped the back fence, then climbed the forked tree beside the creek. My grandmother told me once that Indians would split the tree when it was a sapling to make it grow forked like that, so this place marked a crossroads and was special; she told me I was special since her mother was Cherokee. I found out later that trees naturally grow forked along creek banks, that I didn't have enough Cherokee blood to be a tribal member, and that I was special—just not in the way that Nana meant.

Trace sat in the crook with his back against the trunk and I straddled the offshoot. "This mess tastes like dirt," he said.

"You're not supposed to swallow it." We took turns spitting the brown juice into the creek. The back of my throat started burning and my head was spinning. I lay against the tree, looking up. The last light shifted through the leaves like a kaleidoscope.

"I feel sick," Trace retched, and I reached out to put my hand on his shoulder.

"It's my fault..." He shrugged me away, leaned back against the trunk, and closed his eyes. "You want to go back inside?"

He shook his head. "In a minute."

I watched him. Mother always said Trace had eyelashes that girls would kill for. And his thick eyebrows were like two wooly caterpillars. His skin had a reddish tint underneath the brown. My arms had fine blonde hairs, but his were smooth.

"You alright?" I asked. His eyes were closed. He didn't answer. I moved closer, studying the remnants of a scab on one of his knuckles; the exposed new flesh was pale. I wanted to peel away the rest of the scab. I held my hand up beside his, amazed that the skin under the scab was the same color as my own. Then I noticed that the freckles on my hand were the exact color of his skin. "Hey, Trace," I whispered, tapping his arm. I wanted him to see.

He didn't budge, only groaned. His lips were slightly parted. I was jealous of the thin line of fine hairs above his top lip. I leaned in to see them up close.

"What the fuck?" His eyes fluttered open.

"What? I was seeing..."

"You trying to kiss me or something?"

"Hell no!" I laughed. "Hey, check this out…" I said, wanting to share my revelation.

Um-hmmm. I saw you. You tried to kiss me, you faggot." He pushed so hard I almost fell out of the tree.

I caught up with him as he was climbing the fence.

"Wait," I cried, as he jumped down on the other side, and turned. He looked me in the eyes and, for a split second, I thought he might say "sorry." Instead he said "You make me sick." Then hocked and spat in my face.

I reached across the fence and gripped his arm as tight as I could. When he couldn't wrench free, he punched me in the mouth with his other hand.

My hands went to my face, my mouth filling with blood, as he ran away.

I THOUGHT OF US, earlier that summer, in the musty camper of my father's pickup, how we had broken into the skin of our thumbs with a screwdriver from the toolbox. It wasn't easy, drawing blood with the blunt tip of a Phillips head. I dug at my thumb, twisting the handle until I bled, then handed the screwdriver to Trace. We were both sweating in the camper's smothering heat. I squeezed my thumb to keep the blood flowing until he was ready, then we pressed our thumbs together, grinning. After that, I had stuck my thumb in my mouth to stop the bleeding. It had the same metallic taste of lust and shame.

CLIMBED THE CHAIN link and ran after him. When I reached the street, I wasn't sure which way to run at first, but then I saw him rounding the corner of the block; and though I knew I'd never catch up with him, I still ran until my side cramped, until he'd disappeared altogether. I pictured him running all the way downtown where the stalker in the white truck , in my mind, perpetually cruised the city streets. Through a busted lip I screamed his name three times (which must've sounded, in my unchanged voice, like a girl screaming "Rape") before collapsing on the sidewalk in tears. Between heaves, I sobbed *I'm sorry* and *please come back* as if he could hear me. After I finally quit gasping, I cried in silence till the street lights snapped on, which is right about the time my lip started to throb. Rather, I sensed the ache that had been there all along and reached to touch it—either to assess the damage or lessen the pain. I winced of course, since touching it only made it hurt worse. But I persisted, gently probing the wound from the inside, with my tongue while thinking Trace would never speak to me again.

Time passed this way, so slow I barely noticed how the sound that crickets make replaced the rushing of my heartbeat, how they gave the night a pulse. In the distance, the bell tower struck ten hollow notes. And then a new thought tinged the calm with dread: even worse than never speaking to me again, he'd tell everyone at school what I had done. I felt a tingling, like something crawling, along my hairline as I got up and started towards the Quickie Mart, towards Trace's neighborhood, praying that the man in the white pick-up would come back. Above me, a single bat mobbed the street lamp where the moths swarmed.

The Anatomy of a Slideshow

There is film of us projected on the ceiling—
        how many planets are there again/give me a number,

you tell me about a friend who cannot name the months of the year
        in a correct order, I have a friend who cannot, too.

Look, we are made for each other. A scene: kissing cheeks in

        art gallery corridors, museum windows, streets

all global. I have checked in/out today in so many different countries.
        One year ago we were in Europe together

and in love, do you remember. How can one forget.
        It's easy, you say. I'm nostalgic for frustrating moments,

for casual advances. What can I say for minimalism more than
        I have never said the things you say to me to anyone.

Even you. It gets dark so early these days, you know.

KATIE JEAN SHINKLE

The Abbreviation of Anatomy

Red nails on white ass, there are small pock-mark
        kiss-bruises on my collarbone, maybe I'll come back,

you say, or you can just come here, or we can figure it out,
        I can't think about it now, you are too much.

How to spank
        for pleasure when you don't even understand

what pleasure is in the first place. What is consent but remembering
        a word in a sea of language. Say "candy apple," Say "Sailor M

Say "Q." What does it mean
        to have your name as a safety word. I'm leaving,

you say again, as if I should stop you.
When I touch my neck, I do not wince. What it means to forget how
        to wince.

BENJAMIN S. GROSSBERG

Provender

Meaning *oats, dried peas*.
Meaning *that which is provided*.
As in, an ear attuned to the note
of stress in a voice. As in,
an ear that knows at a word—
a single word uttered on the phone—
to be gentle, to ask. Or,
in proximity, hands that reach
out toward a body, that slide
palms around it for a chest-to-
back embrace that makes a body
straighten, and experience
what a body experiences
when it straightens. In a house
damaged by fire, such support
is called sistering: new beam
affixed to joist, to stud,
inside the walls, the balloon
frame in which flame once raged.
In a house damaged
by carelessness, by years
of blind taking, it is merely
provender: oats, dried peas,
the animal munching noiseless
in its stall, its capacity
to appreciate limited
because it has never
been hungry, or simply
doesn't have that capacity.

There is a play in which
a character, working in a stable,
laments that he expends himself
for *naught but provender*,
and though it jangles the scene,
I am struck by the word's
beauty: from *to provide*, to see
in advance, *provender*—
to see in advance, and make
provision: the care
knotted in it, the forethought,
solicitude: and in the receiver,
the tenderness, perhaps innocence
that is unable to name the provider,
the definition requiring
passive voice, or the comfort,
luxury, the complacency of being
unable to remember, or
unwilling, that a provider
exists at all.
Provender: high value, unvalued,
in a house that has been damaged
by carelessness, by apathy—
a handful of dry peas,
fistful of oats.

PAULA MARTINAC

Dog Gone

FROM WHERE SHE STOOD at the kitchen window, Lena could see the strong shoots of tulips poking up through the garden soil. They were the color of newness, soft and slightly out of focus, and there seemed to be more this spring than in other years. But then, she'd never really counted. Were there nine, ten, more than a dozen? When they bloomed this year, maybe she'd take a count.

"Do you want me to make you some oatmeal?" Trish asked from the counter, where she was finishing her own breakfast while flipping the pages of the morning paper. The gentle swishing sound was comforting and familiar. Trish never seemed to actually read the paper; she just glanced at headlines, sometimes calling them out to Lena as they lingered over breakfast, then flipped the page and scanned some more.

"No," Lena replied. "Thanks."

"I tried that new fruit spread yesterday, the one I found at the co-op? It's really good. Morello cherries - all I can say is, yum. I could make you some toast."

The tulip shoots swayed a little in the morning air. Lena peeled her eyes from them and turned toward the counter.

"Sounds great, but I'm good. Coffee's all I want." Lena raised her mug toward Trish in a weak salute.

Trish took her time folding up the paper, smoothing it out, while they both sipped their coffee. "I wish you'd let me go with you," she said at last. "I mean, this isn't the kind of thing anybody should have to do alone. I could leave work early, get there by two."

"Thanks," Lena said. "But actually, I'm thinking I might not go today."

"But you took the day off!"

"I'll go tomorrow," Lena said, bending over to pet Cody, who lay in a sleepy puddle near her feet. "It's such a beautiful day. And it's going to rain again tomorrow. I thought Cody and me would go for a walk in the park. You know, take advantage of the weather. You'd like that, wouldn't you, boy?" Cody opened his dreamy eyes, his tail thumping a couple of times against the floor, then slipped back into snoozing.

Trish got up from the counter without the rebuke Lena had expected, her slippers flapping against the tile floor. Plates and silverware clacked into the dishwasher. She was looking down at Cody when she finally said, "Well, if you change your mind--"

"Don't worry, I won't," Lena interrupted, immediately wishing she hadn't said it so quickly. It sounded harsh, even to her, yet she couldn't stop the words from coming out of her mouth. Trish nodded once, then padded out. Lena turned toward the window again as her spaniel snored.

CODY'S FAVORITE bench was just to the left of the kids' section of the park. He couldn't walk by it without begging to stop for a sit-and-sniff session, even a brief one. Lena didn't really like to sit in the kids' section, mostly because she didn't have a kid, and Cody was a kid magnet, a little white and brown ball of fur with huge, expressive eyes. But today she gave in to him. "Okay, boy, up," and he jumped onto the bench, his nose immediately tuning in to the cacophony of smells: snacks dropped by kids, other dogs' pee, car exhaust, all against the background of early spring freshness after several days of rain.

They hadn't been there a minute when a red-haired boy about four darted over to them from the gym. Lena glanced around for his parent or guardian, but no one seemed to have an eye out for him, although there were several parents milling about.

"Can I pet your dog?" came the boy's inevitable question.

"Sure," Lena replied.

"I don't have a dog," he said with regret.

She said, "I know," because she could always tell the kids who didn't have animals in their lives by their petting technique. They went for Cody's head with heavy-handed fervor. This one actually grabbed him near his ears and stared him right in the eyes. "What's your name?" the boy cooed, looking so closely and intently into Cody's face that the dog turned away, wriggling uncomfortably on the bench. Lena's hand reached out to guide the boy's pats to a safer place on Cody's torso. "Like this. Not so hard," she directed. "You know, dogs don't like it when you look right at them."

"Why not?"

"They feel threatened... nervous," she explained. "He doesn't know you."

"Oh-h-h," the little boy said, patting the dog's side the way Lena instructed him. After a few moments, she offered, "His name is Cody."

"Co-dee! I love you, Cody!" the boy shrieked, making Cody startle. Lena wanted to say, "Not so loud," but she was beginning to feel like an old crank. She reminded herself that Cody was resilient; he could suffer a little boy's innocent enthusiasm. But still, she wished some parent would come and retrieve him, so she and Cody would have reason to get up and move.

"He looks like Reilly," the boy said suddenly, staring into Cody's face again. Agitated, Lena stood up and edged away from the bench with Cody, but the boy followed, calling after them, "Here, Reilly!"

"I told you, his name is Cody," she reprimanded. "Who is Reilly?"

"Dog on the sign," the boy said, pointing off vaguely.

Lena's stomach clenched. Not only was she saddled with a boy without a guardian, now he was telling her about a lost dog. She'd seen many of those homemade "LOST! Have you seen [dog's name]?" posters, and they always made her furious. If you were careful and responsible, how in the world did you lose a dog?

"Where's your mom?" Lena asked finally, in a tone that was a bit too abrupt.

"At work."

"Then who brought you here?"

The boy indicated the same vague location as the missing dog poster. She started to ask another question, but he suddenly turned and zoomed off down the path, shouting over his shoulder, "Bye, Cody!" Lena watched as a young woman on a cell phone popped out from behind the jungle gym, waving him toward her.

Lena urged Cody toward the tennis courts, where there was a notice board marked "Information." People advertised all sorts of services on homemade flyers - pet sitting, house cleaning, even personal shopping ("Too tired from working all week to shop for Mother's Day? Let ME do it for you!"). A local environmental group was hosting a clean-up day. The tennis court association was throwing a season-opening bash.

And there, at the edge of the board, was the photo of a soulful-looking mutt, some sort of scruffy terrier mix. With his short, pointy ears and square face, he looked absolutely nothing like Cody, except for his white-and-brown coloring. The name "Reilly" appeared above his picture in huge capital letters. Below was the sad truth: "MISSING SINCE MARCH 5. IF FOUND, PLEASE CALL!!! REWARD REWARD REWARD!!! FOR MORE INFO: WWW. WHERESREILLY.BLOGLAND.COM."

Lena found her hand shaking a little as she ripped the last tear-off tab from the bottom of the flyer. She stuffed the contact information into her jacket pocket. "Let's go, boy," she said, and pulled Cody toward their favorite trail.

The woods smelled delicious and new. Cody stopped every couple of feet to grab a whiff of something, and Lena waited patiently, observing the delicate growth on the trees. On days when she was in a hurry, she had to drag Cody along, but today she had nowhere else to be. They would emerge back into the world whenever the woods tired them. For minutes, she stared amazed at an old tree stump that was sprouting a miniature city of fungi and green shoots, while Cody sniffed the stump's base; she thought how she couldn't wait to describe it to Trish.

Movement caught the corner of her eye, and she turned to see a brown-and-white mutt about fifty feet down the trail, watching the two of them in nervous anticipation - Reilly, or if not him, his twin. Or was he slightly smaller? Tugging on Cody's leash, she looked away for a second toward her own dog, who was still busily sniffing. "Let's go, boy," she coaxed. But when she glanced back, the other dog had already gone, evaporated into the woods.

Her fingers grazed the ripped paper in her pocket. She dug deeper inside her jacket for her cell. "Your call has been forwarded to an automatic voice messaging system. At the tone, please record your message."

Lena opened her mouth to speak, but wasn't sure what to say. She disconnected, then dialed again. "Hi, I think I just saw your dog Reilly in Frick Park on Tranquil Trail. Not far from the dog run? About, oh, probably 10:30. He ran away before I could get closer, but he looked a lot like the photo on the flyer." She took in some cool morning air. "You know, I just want to say, it's really bad to let your dog off leash."

After she disconnected, she realized she hadn't left her name or a return number.

THE WEBSITE "Where's Reilly" opened with the same expressive photo of the mutt that was on the flyer, his ears bending slightly backward as if something had just cowered him. His brief life story broke Lena's heart: abuse by a previous owner, a year at the animal shelter, a second owner that returned him, another stint at the shelter, and then the new owners. "We were giving Reilly a new chance at happiness, and then he disappeared!!!" read the text, although it neglected to say how he had vanished on his own. The holes in the story left Lena to fill in her own interpretation: neglectful owner lets dog off-leash in the park, and he's never seen again.

"Hey." Trish was the in door of the study, staring at her quizzically.

"Oh, hi. When'd you get home?"

"I've been calling out 'I'm home' for, like, ten minutes."

"Sorry. I got engrossed."

Lena returned to the site's home page and offered Trish a look. "I saw this dog in the park. He's lost. I called and left a message for the owner. You know I can't stand it when people let their dogs off leash!"

Trish laid a patient hand on her shoulder. "They do it all the time." There had been so many things Lena wanted to tell her partner about her walk with Cody, but she forgot them now. "Why's it upset you so much?"

"I'm not that upset," Lena protested.

"You are. I can hear it in your voice."

After almost 20 years together, she still tried to fool Trish sometimes. It never worked. "He's a sad-looking little guy. I'm worried that he's hungry. And his story is so infuriating."

Trish was rubbing both of her shoulders now, and she leaned gratefully into the massage. "That's quite a knot you've got going there," Trish remarked. After more kneading, she continued, "Did you call to reschedule?"

"Shit! I knew I forgot something." It wasn't a lie; after seeing Reilly in the park, Lena had shuffled everything else to the back of her mind.

"Lena…"

"I know, I know," she said, shrugging off Trish's hands. "I'll do it tomorrow. First thing."

D OLEFUL IRISH MUSIC filled the car, the moan of uilleann pipes - a local band Lena had heard once at an arts festival, whose songs she couldn't get out of her mind. Trish found it harsh and whiny - "It's just so depressing," she complained - so Lena only played the CD while driving. One track in particular she repeated again and again, to hear the way the pipes started soft, alone, then joined with fiddle and hammered dulcimer. She was hitting the track button a third time when she saw him up ahead on the side of the road, in front of a stand of wild forsythia, ready to dart into traffic.

She wished she had a copy of the flyer, but she knew from the quick, dull thump in her stomach that it was Reilly - the coloring, the gait, one pointed ear up and the other down, questioning or perplexed. What was he doing way out here? He looked scraggly and tired of making his own way in the world when he should have been at home, sprawled carelessly on his bed.

Lena pulled over abruptly and without signaling, causing a Toyota driver behind her to lean on his horn as he swerved away from rear-ending her. She gave him the finger as he yelled "Are you fuckin' crazy, lady?" through the passenger window, waving his fist at her in rage. It was a stupid, childish gesture on her part, she knew, especially when the near-accident was all her fault; a risky one, too, if the driver decided to stop and confront her face to face. Luckily, he drove on, maybe stunned by such audacity from a woman with salt-and-pepper hair.

Lena turned to the spot where Reilly had stood like a deer in headlights, but he had vanished once again into the brush. She walked a few yards back and forth, trying to see signs of movement. Aside from a squirrel busy with an acorn, everything was still. Back in her car, she leaned heavily on the steering wheel, her heart racing.

S HE WAS ALMOST twenty minutes late when she signed in at the front desk. Under "Reason for Visit," she printed "see Kathy Welch" instead of the usual "visit James Pruitt." In her hurry, she made a mistake and spelled it "Welsh," the crossed it out and corrected it. "She'll be right with you," the receptionist said.

The space where she waited for Kathy was a small activities room with a kitchenette at one end where just last month Lena and her father had sat together and watched as the bubbly young social director mixed up a batch of chocolate chip cookies, explaining her actions as she went along, and then passed them out, warm and chewy, to the residents. Lena privately called her "Julie Your Cruise Director," mostly to make Trish laugh; her nametag clearly read "BRITTANY" in huge block letters. Lena had been the only person in the room - besides Brittany, that is - under 80.

When Lena was leaving, Brittany pulled her aside and thanked her for coming. "We try to make healthy snacks, too, y'know. Like, I've got a killer recipe for blueberry muffins with tofu, but we gotta wait for blueberry season," she explained. To Lena, the thought of making her 89-year-old father - for whom the phrase "meat and potatoes" had surely been invented - eat tofu verged on elder abuse.

A small clump of white-haired women sat one table over from Lena, not doing much of anything, not even talking to each other. Two of them were, in fact, dozing off. One turned to Lena when she sat down and waved, and Lena shyly waved back. "He's not doin' too hot, is he?" the woman called down to her after a few seconds.

"No," Lena replied. "He's not." They all know, she thought.

The woman shook her head and returned to sitting in silence with the others.

Kathy Welch whirled into the room carrying a file folder, her glasses hanging from a beaded cord around her neck. "Hi Kathy!" the woman who waved at Lena shouted out happily.

"Hello, Mrs. Mancini!" Kathy returned. "How are you feeling today?"

"My arm's a little sore," Mrs. Mancini replied, a grave look clouding her face as she touched her right shoulder.

"Well, I'll have Rita take a look," Kathy said, pulling out the chair next to Lena and positioning her glasses on the bridge of her nose.

"Right after I'm done here. How's that sound?" Mrs. Mancini nodded and slowly let her hand drop away from the shoulder.

"Lena, there are just a couple of papers that need your signature," Kathy said, turning her attention to the folder and lowering her voice. "This first one says that I've clearly explained the hospice program to you." She edged a sheet toward Lena with an X at the spot to sign, and Lena scrawled her name quickly. "This one says that you have the authority to make this decision." The sheet was a blur, but she signed. "And this one gives us the go-ahead to start the program."

Lena's hand hesitated over the sheet. "When will it start?" she asked.

"As soon as you sign," Kathy replied. "Well, as soon as I get the papers to the nurses on your father's floor. They'll make him as comfortable as possible."

Lena tried to sign a third time, but the pen skipped and was out of ink. It scratched a small tear in the paper. "Damn it!" she said, tears at the corners of her eyes.

An image of her father, young, shot into Lena's mind. He was building a birdhouse for the back yard, a small but faithful replica of their own house; when finished, it would be complete down to a tiny street address sign on the front. As Lena watched intently, passing him nails from a pile he'd set up for her, he accidentally caught his thumb with the hammer. "Damn it! Goddamn hammer!" her father screamed, jumping up from his worktable, his faced laced with pain. Lena stood up, too, her eyes clouding over in fear. "Daddy, Daddy!" she cried out. Her father tucked his stinging thumb quickly under his arm and out of her line of vision. "I mean, doggone hammer!"

Kathy produced a felt-tip pen, and touched a cool hand to Lena's wrist, bringing her back to the room. The third signature came out heavier, more pronounced than the others.

"Unless you have questions, that about does it," Kathy said.

"No, I'm good," Lena replied, her voice quivering slightly on the word "good."

"You've done the right thing, Lena," Kathy assured her, even though she hadn't asked her opinion. "I know your brother didn't approve. But it's the right thing."

"My brother…" she began, but didn't finish. What could she say about a 50-year-old man who took no responsibility for their father's care? He hadn't even flown in to say goodbye. "The old man will outlive us both," was his reasoning.

Lena stood to go. "I think I'll go see him now," she said. When she was in the hallway, trying to breathe, she realized that she should have waved goodbye to Mrs. Mancini.

S OMEONE HAD PLACED a CD player in her father's room, and classical music floated in a soft, soothing background to her visit. The music was unrecognizable to her; she had no ear for classical, and only knew the "greatest hits." Sitting down beside the bed, Lena thought that playing classical music for her dad was similar to giving him tofu muffins. "I'll bring you some Peggy Lee next time, Dad," she said. She laid a hand on his head, which was cool, but he didn't wake up from his bottomless sleep.

Thinking back, she wondered how long he had been getting ready for this deep rest. Just a week earlier, he was waiting for her in the lounge, hands feeling for the wheels of his chair, ready to roll. But the strength in his arms had been gone for a while, and he relied on her to move him around.

"Oh, good, it's you," he said. "I was wondering how I was gonna get change for the bus."

"What bus, Dad?"

"The bus to Woods Run. They took all my change. Can you loan me some? I'll pay you back."

"Sure, Dad," Lena said, not bothering to contradict him. He hadn't had any money since he arrived at the nursing home six months ago.

"Good," he said, with a deep breath of relief. "That's good. I don't want the driver to pass me by."

Now she wished she had known that was the last time she'd hear his voice; she would have listened to it more carefully. She stroked his head again and told him she'd be back soon.

In the parking lot, Lena laid her head on the steering wheel and sobbed.

T HE WOMAN PICKED UP on the third ring with the wary voice of someone who doesn't recognize the caller ID number. "Hello?"

"Oh, hi!" Lena said, fiddling with the stapler on her desk. She had waited until her boss was out of the office to make the call. He had an unnerving habit of padding up behind her without warning and borrowing things from her desk, like a pen or scissors, even though his own desk was well-stocked. "You don't know me. I left you a message yesterday about your dog, Reilly? About seeing him in Frick Park?"

"You the one who yelled at me for letting him off leash?"

Lena ignored the question, which was peppered with irritation. "I just wanted to tell you I saw him again this afternoon. Out near Highland Park. I don't know how he got there, but--"

"That wasn't my Reilly," the woman snapped.

"It looked like him. I'm almost positive. I didn't have the flyer with me, but--"

"We found Reilly about a week ago."

Air rushed into Lena's lungs. "You got him back!"

The long pause was an eerie prelude to the woman's next words. "No," she said, a tremor in her voice. "He got hit by a car. We had to… put him down."

"Oh, God, I'm so sorry," Lena said, and the hard knot she felt earlier in her stomach returned. "Really, I am. I didn't realize. It must be someone else's lost dog I've been seeing everywhere. Someone should probably take your flyers down."

The woman's voice fractured. "Look, whoever you are, I don't appreciate all these calls! You don't know anything! For your information, Reilly dug his way out of our yard, right under the fence. So just leave me alone! My dog's dead, understand? Take the damn flyers down yourself!"

Lena sat with the cell phone pressed heavily to her ear, then snapped it closed.

T HE TREATS WERE the premium, all-natural kind she bought for Cody, the Turkey 'n' Taters flavor he went especially nuts for and would do any trick to get. Lena grabbed the bag from the front seat and got out of her car. It had been hours since she'd seen the dog that looked like Reilly, but maybe he was still in the vicinity, hungry and trying to find his way home.

"Here, boy! Treats! Yum - turkey!"

Lena tried to ignore that several drivers in passing cars stared at her. One woman with two young children in the back seat actually slowed down and called to her from the window, "Are you all right?"

"Fine, thanks."

The woman looked unconvinced, and pulled off with a jerky, hesitant movement.

"Turkey!" Lena beckoned a few more times before she got in the car again and drove home.

T RISH'S VOICE INTERRUPTED the sound of forks on plates. Her hand reached over to Lena's and covered it.

"You did the right thing," she said.

Lena looked up, startled; she had forgotten where she was. The plate in front of her was still mostly full, a bite taken here and there, broccoli florets pushed from side to side.

"What?" she asked, wondering how Trish knew that she had called Reilly's owner.

"You dad," Trish replied, a sliver of irritation in her voice.

"I wasn't really thinking about him," Lena said, and it was true. "I keep seeing this lost dog everywhere, but when I go to him, he runs away. And when I called the number on the flyer, the woman said that her dog Reilly got hit by a car. But somebody's dog is still out there, lost, and wandering around hungry."

Trish finished her meal and wiped her mouth slowly with her napkin, then laid it on the table, taking the time, it seemed, to measure her words. "What do you say we both have a mental health day tomorrow and take the bikes to Ohiopyle? I'll ask Grace to walk Cody for us." She paused again, eyes searching Lena's face. "We haven't been in a long time."

"I just took a day off," Lena reminded her, "and I'm kind of behind at work."

Trish deflated, her shoulders and chest caving in. "You've been shutting me out all week," she said, her voice on the verge of cracking. "Ever since the doctor recommended hospice."

"I'm sorry," Lena said.

"Don't say you're sorry," Trish snapped, standing and beginning to clear her place. "I don't want you to be sorry. I just don't want you to shut me out."

Lena nodded, biting back another apology.

S HE WAS JUST SLIDING off into sleep when the phone rang. At first, she thought it was the alarm, and slapped at it to shut it up. But then there was a flood of bright light, Cody was stretching at the bottom of the bed, and Trish's voice rose through the fog: "Hello. Yes, yes, she's here. Just a minute, please." Trish put the receiver into Lena's hand, mouthing the words, "It's the nurse."

Lena listened to the unfamiliar, disembodied voice on the other end, not catching the name attached to it. Night nurse. Your father. Vital signs. Change. Morning. "You might want to come."

"Right now?" Lena asked. "It's almost midnight."

"It's up to you," the nurse replied, in the frustratingly cautious way of medical personnel.

"Let me ask you this," Lena said slowly. "If he were your father, what would you do?"

"I'd come," said the nurse, without hesitation.

"Thank you. I'll be there soon."

Lena handed the phone back to Trish and hopped out of bed, pulling on the clothes she'd discarded just an hour earlier. "It sounds like he might not make it through the night," she said. "I had no idea it would happen this soon. I have to go."

Trish watched her dress, petting Cody absently, her eyes much larger than their normal size. "What about me?" she asked as Lena bent over to tie her shoes.

"I don't know how long I'll be," Lena hesitated. "There's Cody…"

"We could take both cars," Trish suggested.

"Okay," Lena agreed.

N EVER KNOW HOW much I love you, never know how much I care,'" sang Peggy Lee in her most seductive song - her father's favorite, the hint of lust and longing heavy in both the tune and lyrics. When Lena was little, he would play it again and again, whistling in perfect harmony as Peggy sang. Sometimes, he pulled Lena's mother into a sexy slow dance that was both thrilling and embarrassing to watch as she giggled in his arms. "'You give me fever…'"

Trish and Lena took chairs across from each other and held his hands. There was both too little and too much to say. "Trish and I are here, Daddy," Lena said. "We're doing great. Cody wanted to come, too, but they won't let him in." An image of her father with Cody standing in his lap, paws wrapped around her dad's neck while the dog delivered sloppy kisses, filtered into Lena's mind and made her smile. "It's okay to go. You can get on the bus and be with Mommy."

Within just a few minutes, her father's breathing became slower, more erratic. Lena had no firsthand experience with death. Her mother had passed away quickly, from a stroke, while Lena was at work. This was a scene out of a tearjerker movie, and yet, amazingly, Lena had no idea which scene came next.

His breathing stopped suddenly, and then, after several minutes in which she and Trish shot anxious looks at each other, started up again. There were a couple of brief, hollow inhalations, and then nothing more.

"I think that may be... I'll get the nurse," Trish offered.

Lena leaned in toward his nose, trying to feel the slightest wisp of life. "Dad, you still there?" she whispered, although she knew that he wasn't. Lena pressed her lips to the papery skin of his cheek.

W E'LL BE EATING tuna casserole for weeks," Trish announced, pondering the contents of the refrigerator. "Marianne's makes three. I was hoping for some of her famous ginger-carrot soup instead."

Lena turned reluctantly from the kitchen window. The first tulip heads had appeared overnight, poking up through the stand of muted leaves. The sun fell on them softly, making her want to hover over them, detect each little change.

"Good thing we like tuna casserole," Lena said.

They stared at each other for a moment, longtime partners without words at the ready, who knew almost everything there was to know about each other. "That dress looks fantastic on you," Trish said finally. Lena had bought it the day before, during a frantic trip to the mall because all of her clothes seemed wrong for a funeral.

"That wasn't the look I was going for," Lena said, worried. "I better change."

"Sweetie, no," Trish said, putting an arm around her. "You don't have to change. It's totally fine for the funeral. Your dad would like it. I just meant... never mind."

"You sure?"

"Poz." Trish squeezed her shoulder, but Lena was aware of being stiff to the touch. "I was wondering," Trish said slowly, "do you want me to call the bereavement counselor, the one in the brochure? We could both go."

"It's okay, Trish," she said. "I can call myself."

"I know you 'can,'" Trish replied. "But I don't think you will."

"I'm not sure I need to," she hesitated. What could the counselor possibly help her feel that she didn't already?

"Lena," Trish said, shifting into her "parent" voice, "I'm pretty sure you do."

Lena didn't mean to detonate. She just didn't want to talk about tuna casserole, or look fantastic in a dress, or be told what to do. She wanted to lie down on the bed and hug Cody and listen to Peggy Lee and cry. "Stop trying to control my grief!" she said, pulling roughly out of Trish's embrace.

She was instantly sorry; Trish looked like she'd been slapped. Cody, who had been lying quietly in the corner, popped up, stared at Lena, then at Trish, and began to pace between them nervously. Trish burst into big, hot tears that made Lena draw her into her arms.

"I didn't mean it," Lena said, avoiding the empty word "sorry." "I so much didn't mean it. Thank you for offering to call the counselor."

"I'm sad, too, y'know," Trish said, through gulps of air. "I miss the old guy, the way he called me 'doll.'"

Lena stroked her back, and they held onto each other until Cody, whimpering, forced his way between them, making them both start laughing in spite of everything.

THE FLYER FOR REILLY was still on the notice board in the park, tattered and yellowed from the elements. She wasn't sure how long she'd been staring at it before Cody began coaxing her away, pulling determinedly at the leash, anxious to get started on their walk.

"Okay, okay," she said. But as she turned to go, her eyes fell on a new flyer at the bottom of the board, this one with the upturned face of another terrier mix, smaller than Reilly, staring back at her. Beneath the color photo was the bold-faced word "FOUND!" and a brief and affecting story of how Zoey had made her way home, hungry and scared, after several harrowing days living on the streets. "Thanks to the many NEIGHBORS who PHONED us with Zoey sightings ALL over the East End - you saved her LIFE!" The randomly capitalized words made the flyer look like a child had created it. Strolling off down the trail with Cody, Lena thought how right it seemed that "life" was one of them.

ANGELO NIKOLOPOULOS

Dudes on Campus

Berkeley, CA

My cherry lips have often kiss'd
thy stones too, P and T—big whoop.

When the Campanile chimes its bells at noon
we bottleneck beneath Sather Gate

against elbows and flyers and our blatant youth.
It's all very tiring,

the self made public and obvious.
Who needs eucalyptus groves and Strawberry Creek?

I detest the sun's etiquette.
Let's celebrate the basement bathroom instead

where we wait in that darkened bower,
creaky ship hull, pressed against

the stall's buffered edge.
Until there it comes, through the opening,

dumb and quiet. Where it's easy to adore most
that which goes unsaid—

loving drape of silence, anonymity's pledge—
to put yourself

through a chink in a wall and have kindness
greet you on the other end.

ANGELO NIKOLOPOULOS

Breeder Fever: Auditions

for Alice Fulton

It was different in high school. We'd make
the best of ten minutes and puberty
with our histamines, swapping saliva until
the tongue became instrument: The Slap
Machine. The Hurricane. The Froth Maker.
His mouth made me sick and I did nothing
but savor each symptom: the fever chills,
reddened nose blush, the smooth Amoxicillin
down the throat like a pink ribbon. Until
the virus spread—first to mother, then father,
then to brother—love's house of strange
invalids, each in our delicate misery.
Because to touch each other might break us,
we'd breathe the same air and hold it in our
chambered lungs, as if feeling were contagious.
I almost admired it. I almost wrote despised.

JULIE MARIE WADE

When I Was Straight

Everything came to me vicariously—a promise,
a post-script, a preview of coming attractions.

Desire a quiet rumor that rippled through the halls.

At the cinema, someone always paid for popcorn, a soda
with two straws, little licorice candies.

I loved to sit in the back row & watch
till all the credits rolled.

"You have a gift," the blond boy said, "for stalling."

Later, in a twin bed in a college dorm, I spoke without thinking—
"I like you. Let's get this over with."

His pink mouth amazed, so wide & round.
"Did you hear what you just said?" he asked.

I hadn't been listening.

JULIE MARIE WADE

When I Was Straight

You were straight, too, & we were
all straight together like sticks on the ground,
or a plain staff of parallel lines longing to be made into music.

We built a campfire in the park & sat boy-girl-boy-girl
around it, toasting marshmallows & telling a story.
Someone had a harmonica & knew how to play.

The story we always told was how the continents used to
fit together like a jigsaw puzzle, so big you had to put the leaf
in the center of the table if you wanted to see it complete.

Why were they like that? we wondered.
How had they come to be undone?

Then, there was the father who said, "We must never question
God's plan," & the mother who, daubing the honey-sweet
perfume under her ears, instructed us to listen to the father.

When I was straight, you were straight, too, & we were
ordinary & exceptional & always a little afraid.
We saw geese flying overheard & worried at their wild skein.

Why were they like that? we wondered.
Had their teachers not taught them to single file?

We learned cursive on dashed lines that formed the letters for you.
We played connect the dots but used the sharp-edge to be sure.
Hands were washed before dinner, & prayers were said before bed.

Then, the father handed you a bag of pegs, the mother a basket of
clothes. "Someday you will grow up & follow in our footsteps,"
they said. Skeptical, you studied their shoes.

When I was straight, you were straight, too, & we were
all straight together like sheets on the line. Each perfect crease &
corner. Mostly still, with a slight billow from time to time.

No one was otherwise, you see.
No one had been told another story.

What happened next remained a matter of speculation. The administration accepted what Mr. Franklin told them. He'd been careless.

VIET DINH

Something Here Will Eventually Have to Explode

r. Franklin started each school year with a horror story: *Once upon a time, there was this young girl with beautiful blonde hair…* None of his students listened, of course, but it was customary, like a handshake. He pointed out the emergency shower and the eyewash station. Green deposits, oxidized copper from the pipes, had caked onto the nozzles which were tested only once a year. Mr. Franklin wondered if the drains in the bottom of the floor actually lead anywhere. *One day, she leaned too close to her Bunsen burner…*

"I suggest you ladies tie your hair back before working over an open flame," he said. "You too, Mr. Jeffers." Brad Jeffers, famous throughout Clarkfield High for his last-quarter drive to take the football team to finals, shook his shoulder-length hair to little splatters of laughter radiating around him. Already, Mr. Franklin could foretell the grades of every student in the room: Brad would study earnestly and half-heartedly land a B, more out of pity than effort. Cassie, in the front row, had the hungry intensity of an A student refusing to earn anything less. Mark and Seth, fellow football players who had followed Brad into class, were destined for Cs. "You'll be surprised how quickly human hair burns. Once the burning hair reaches the follicle, it scars, and no hair will ever grow there again."

The chain for the emergency shower ended with metal rod bent into a triangle. Mr. Franklin batted it absent-mindedly. Which story next: acid splashed into the eyes or flaming shirt sleeves?

"How do we know if the shower works?" Brad asked.

Most of these students he'd had as sophomores in Earth Science, the next-to-last required science class in the curriculum. From there, students either chose his class—real chemistry—or Mr. Wilbur's Chemistry in Our Everyday Lives, a series of filmstrips and exercises out of the book. Mr. Wilbur's face bore the Minnesota landscape: dark creases in a flat plain. Once at the grocery store, he spotted Mr. Wilbur stacking cartons of beer into his cart. Mr. Wilbur popped open a can, right in the aisle. "Just one drink a day until retirement," Mr. Wilbur said to him. "Cheers."

The class awaited his answer. "Well, Brad" Mr. Franklin said, "if you want to try it out, go ahead."

Brad half-rose from his desk, as if taking Mr. Franklin's challenge at face value. It was then that Mr. Franklin noticed the young man sitting behind Brad. He cross-checked his roster. Richard Lamberton. He disappeared behind Brad's blonde bulk like a shadow. He wore a t-shirt with a cracked Dukes of Hazzard iron-on decal—a shirt that would have commanded a hefty price at the vintage stores lining Clark Street back in Chicago. Indeed, that shirt would have been a status symbol in Mr. Franklin's own high school days.

But Richard wore it without irony, and he twisted his long, lanky body as if comfort were forever out of reach. Red exclamations of acne dotted his face. And while Brad's unkempt hair had been painstakingly molded, Richard's fell limp from his scalp, a brown mass, shiny with oil.

Mr. Franklin wondered: *Had he ever been that awkward?* He must have been. His own face had been as fine and smooth as paper until his junior year, but as soon as the first fine hairs sprouted on his upper lip, he took his father's straight razor and scraped away layers of skin until his mouth was raw. He'd heard that the more you shaved, the thicker the hairs grew back. He measured the thickness of his lip hair with a caliper, jotting the results in a notebook the way other boys tracked penis development. And despite the jokes—that he'd brown nosed so much it left a mark, that he had joined the Village People fan club—the strands poking through his pores grew progressively darker, denser. By graduation, the moustache almost obscured his entire mouth.

And while the other students politely tittered at the run-in with Brad, Richard remained silent, his arms crossed. It wasn't the carefully crafted nonchalance that Mark and Seth wore like cocked baseball caps. Instead, Richard was already somewhere far away.

Indeed, Clarkfield wasn't someplace Mr. Franklin thought he'd end up in. The town was smaller than anyplace he'd ever lived—perhaps smaller than anything he'd driven through. But Marcia had grown up here, and her parents lived nearby. It was an escape from Chicago, and the Lyons County School District was eager to recruit new science teachers.

After two years, he'd grown accustomed to the new raft of excused absences—harvest time, State Fair, rehab at Hazleton—but not to his own ubiquity. Everywhere he went, he ran into students. Bagging his groceries at Hy-Vee, driving the tractor that half-blocked the highway, walking down the two blocks that constituted Main Street. He'd managed, for a time, to attain a comfortable anonymity in Chicago, but here, people continually congratulated him on Marcia's pregnancy. When he and Marcia walked through Wal-Mart, he felt the need to put his arm around her shoulder, as if announcing, *Look what I did!*

Marcia enjoyed the spotlight more than he did. People remembered her from way back, as if anything outside of Clarkfield ceased to exist. *We knew you'd be back some day,* they said, and Mr. Franklin knew that he should have been grateful for how welcoming they were. Sioux Falls was 90 minutes away; Minneapolis, three hours, and if he were the last bastion of big city suspicion and paranoia, so be it. He'd earned the right.

H IS FIRST RUN-IN with Richard came two days before Thanks-
giving break, the pre-vacation dead zone. He'd been preparing a
lecture about the narcoleptic affects of the tryptophan in turkey when
he noticed how Richard's desk seemed dingier than its neighbors.
Upon closer inspection, the entire desk was covered in writing—small,
in pencil, smudged and graceless. The hard plastic surface had become
marbled and gray, like petrified wood.

> *Hi, who sits here?*
> *This is Clint.*
> *Hi I'm Doreen.*
> *So what do you think of this town?*
> *It sucks.*
> *Yeah I can't wait to get out.*

The conversation continued down the armrest. It was like a year-
book: sentiments from people—already forgotten—filling every
conceivable space.

Who sits here? Such a simple question: he knew exactly who sat
there. Clint, physics. Doreen, earth science, well on her way to having
her likeness carved in butter at the State Fair. Luke, general science,
who didn't care about science beyond how the nitrogen cycle affected
crops. And Richard. This desk-turned-confessional must have gone
on all semester. Doreen wrote about her break-up; Clint about how
he wanted to play lacrosse for the U of M, but his parents couldn't
afford tuition.

During the next class, he stood behind Richard. If he hadn't been
looking, it might have seemed as if Richard were writing his lab report,
but Richard was writing *through* the holes of his notebook paper.
The letters in the aperture emerged deflated, the a's and o's flattened
and exhausted. As far as Mr. Franklin could remember, Richard had
never raised his hand. During labs, he was the partner who weighed
materials and took notes, but never approached the Bunsen burner.

Mr. Franklin came up behind him. "What are you doing?"

Richard stopped. In a low, quiet voice, he said, "Writing."

"Shouldn't you be writing up your lab?"

"It's done," he said, pulling out another sheet of paper. He handed it to Mr. Franklin, who could tell at a glance that it was complete and correct. But it wasn't absolution.

"I want to see you after school," he said. But what Mr. Franklin really wanted was to read what Richard had written, but he was already smearing away the words with his finger.

SEVENTH PERIOD WAS Mr. Franklin's student-free planning period, but he rarely planned. Instead, he took advantage of the school's swimming pool, the only one in a ten-town radius. It saved on the YMCA membership twenty miles south in Marshall and afforded him time to think. The swimming teacher was only part-time and left after fourth period. After that, the pool was off-limits to students. But not to him.

He thought of possible punishments for Richard. *I can make him rinse test tubes.* The air, sharp with vaporized chlorine, stung his nostrils. He remembered the heat wave in Chicago five years ago, how the public pools were saturated with people, how the water roiled from the presence of all those bodies. Here, in Clarkfield, the surface of the pool was completely undisturbed. He could see straight to the bottom. Overhead, the skylights were covered with a coat of snow. Mr. Franklin almost felt bad for Richard. In real life, Clint and Doreen wouldn't have given him the time of day. He'd known people like that—false friends, backstabbers.

The punishment should fit the crime, he thought.

After seventh period, Richard came into the classroom wearing his backpack like a hump. Mr. Franklin wanted to shake him and say, *Snap out of it already!*

"Are you bored in class, Richard?"

He shook his head.

"Well, I'd like it if you'd actually pay attention."

"I'm sorry." Richard's voice was meek and cracked, as if he'd already worn the apology thin.

Mr. Franklin gestured to a Windex bottle and a handful of brown paper towels. "I'd like you to clean all the desks," he said. "Thoroughly."

Richard started at his own desk, obliterating the discussion with a squirt and a wipe. Mr. Franklin had been prepared to handle anger. But resignation—this troubled him. Richard didn't pause to read what Mr. Franklin had written on each desk: *You are responsible for your actions. Please use your time wisely. Apply yourself!* He worked robotically, as if he had been a janitor all his life.

At one desk towards the back of the classroom, Richard scrubbed until the paper towel fell apart into maggoty pieces. He kept his chin near to his chest, as if concentrating on the words.

"I can't seem to get this," he finally said.

Mr. Franklin walked back. Someone had gouged *Mr. Franklin is a cocksucker* into the plastic with a pocketknife. The valley of each letter was filled with black ink. The sentiment was so crude. It was as if the desk itself resented him.

Heat rose into his face. "Just—" He wondered who had written it, who had read it. "Just leave it." He took the Windex bottle from Richard and sprayed the words until they bled. Mr. Franklin's moustache grew damp from sweat. Richard held his backpack by the arm straps, awaiting further instructions. With his fingernail, he scraped hardened ink out of the grooves, but the words remained, permanent as a tattoo.

When all his efforts had failed, Mr. Franklin said, as calmly as possible, "You may go now." He still had self-control—and sometimes it felt as if self-control was all he ever had.

I'm sorry, Richard mumbled, and Mr. Franklin continued his efforts to erase the words.

M R. FRANKLIN'S INFAMOUS periodic table test came two weeks later. No one had ever aced the test, but this year's responses seemed particularly bad. Cs = Caesarium? Brad wrote that, bless his heart. Cassie earned 100% but had missed the extra credit identifications: Rg and Ks.

Richard, however—he actually got them right. He knew roentegenium—a feat that required actual research—and for Ks: "no such element." Mr. Franklin put Richard's test on the top of the stack and scratched the end of his moustache. He wrote, in red, *Perfect!* The cheer felt forced, like applause after a spanking.

He's showing off, Mr. Franklin thought, but would he have done any differently?

Mrs. Groteluschen knocked on his door, waving a sheet of paper.

Mr. Franklin shuffled Richard's paper to the bottom of the pile. "Is it me, or are the students getting dumber?" he asked.

"It's you," she said. She was the grande dame of Clarkfield High—40 years and counting. The administration waited each year for her to announce her retirement, but she insisted, *They'll carry me out of this school in a pine box.* "The ignorance stays constant, but your patience disappears bit by bit. Speaking of which—" She slapped the paper in front of him, palm-down. "Here are the nominees for the National Honor Society. Do you want to rubber stamp them now, or do you want to read through them?"

From between her fingers, he saw Richard's name.

"If I don't want to recommend a student," he said, "what happens?"

"Then they don't get in," she replied. "They can still get in next year."

He circled Richard's name. "I had a run-in with him."

"What kind?"

"Disciplinary."

"It's up to you," she said.

"What's he like in your class?"

"Quiet." She shrugged. "But he can diagram sentences like a madman."

"What do you know about him?"

"Transfer, I think. From the Twin Cities. His father works at Schwann's, I bet. Like everyone else in this godforsaken town."

Other than the desk incident, there was no reason not to recommend Richard. But actions have consequences, even here in Clarkfield. He remembered Marcia staring at him, after he was suspended from his job in Chicago. The kitchen table was a vast gulf. He wondered what she was thinking, and she looked at him as if she already knew what he was thinking. Richard sometimes looked at him the same way, but instead of anger there was—complacency. Complicity.

"I don't think I can recommend him," he said. And Mrs. Groteluschen simply nodded.

That night, he asked Marcia what she would have done. She pursed her lips.

"Oh, it doesn't matter what I think," she said.

"It matters to me."

"Well," she said. "In that case, I think you did the right thing."

"Thought so," he said. But he was pretty sure that she was wrong.

JUST BEFORE THE end of Christmas break, he and Marcia made the six-hour round-trip drive to the Mall of America, braving black-iced highways for maternity clothes. The corn and soy fields—verdant and imposing during summer—were razed and smothered beneath snow. Black patches of earth broke through the white crust like scabs, but otherwise, the land was monotone, expansive. Twin tracks of Ski-Doos crisscrossed the snow but always ended in ditches or half-collapsed barns. Above them, the sky was concrete grey, as if it had been paved over, and sometimes the snow that fell was like rain, and sometimes the rain that fell was like snow. The small towns dotting the road made him ache. He couldn't imagine living in such isolation. Then he remembered: it was already happening.

That night, he went to bed with an aching back and dreamt of

Richard. In his dream, Richard was St. Patrick, pounding the ground with his stick. But instead of driving out the snakes, he'd simply drove them deep into hiding. They burrowed into holes, behind rocks, into crevasses hidden by scrub and brush, curled up, waiting for the right moment to strike.

Once school started again, the students acted as if they'd been roused from hibernation. They grumbled about the slightest assignment and seemed steadfast in their refusal to learn. He spent a full three days on Bohr's model—*Bohr*, for God's sake, the scientific equivalent of training wheels.

He retreated to the pool more and more. There, the cavernous space was deathly quiet. Underwater, only the sound he heard was the rush of water past his ears as his limbs meet the warm resistance. One afternoon in February, as he finished his laps, slightly breathless, eyes burning, and he saw a dark figure in the concrete bleachers. When his vision cleared, he saw that it was Richard, elbows on his knees. How long had he been watching? Above them, the skylights were pregnant with condensation.

"Sorry to bother you, Mr. Franklin," Richard said. He walked to the edge of the pool and squatted at the edge.

"Can I help you?" Mr. Franklin's arms, exposed to the air, prickled with goosebumps. He didn't like feeling as naked as he did. He pushed off the wall and tread water. His lower torso, refracted by ripples, seemed everywhere at once.

"Mrs. Groteluschen told me that you're qualified to teach AP Chemistry."

"I am." He'd taught AP Chemistry in Chicago, but here in Minnesota, he couldn't drum up enough interest to fill a class. He missed teaching it—it was tons better than Earth Science.

"If I wanted to take the AP test next year, could I do an independent study with you?"

For a moment, he wondered if Mrs. Groteluschen had put Richard up to this. But he chided himself for being cynical, suspicious. Richard had an intense gaze, as if trying to part the water by star-

ing at it. To have a student actually interested in chemistry… Mr.
Franklin remembered his own interest long ago, how the world could
be reduced to simple interactions and equations. How variables and
constants ordered the universe. How the mathematical elegance of
shells and subshells made sense of chaos.

"Bohr's model is actually very imprecise, you know," he said. The
denim of Richard's jeans looked perilously thin. The outlines of the
iron-on patches holding the fabric together were obvious. "Don't you
have a class this period?"

Richard shook his head.

"Then why don't you go home early?"

"I have to wait for the bus."

He couldn't imagine how anyone could live in rural Minnesota
without a car. "So what do you do for seventh period?"

"Homework. Or I hang out in the library."

Mr. Franklin paddled to the edge of the pool, grasped the wet
tiles with his fingers. "Well, if you're not doing anything," he said.
His hands were inches from Richard's feet. Richard didn't move.
"Would you like to be my student assistant?"

"Really?"

"It's nothing big. You can count it towards—" He was about to
say *towards the community service component of National Honor Society*,
but caught himself. "It'll be good experience."

"Sure," Richard said.

Mr. Franklin pulled himself out of the pool and extended his
hand. His trunks clung to his thighs, and water trickled down his
legs. He shivered as Richard shook his hand.

"I'll see you tomorrow," Richard said, but he didn't leave. Mr.
Franklin tipped his head to drain his ears. Chlorine in his moustache.
Richard's smile consumed his entire face, and Mr. Franklin wiped
droplets off his arms, out of his hair.

"I should go change," he said, finally, and Richard nodded and
stood stock-still as Mr. Franklin retreated into the locker room.

M R. FRANKLIN HAD had a student assistant once before, in Chicago. James hadn't been exemplary—he just needed extra encouragement, and Mr. Franklin thought that being an assistant would provide that extra push. James, handsome and proud of it, hung out with the other handsome students—none of whom mustered enough effort to overcome a C. So the day the principal informed him that they needed to have a sixth-period meeting with him regarding a student, he assumed it was a routine academic probation issue. And just as he was finishing fifth-period, a man with a face as thick as a cinderblock stormed in. *You Joe Franklin?* the man demanded, and before he could answer, the man balled a fist and punched him in the face. Mr. Franklin stumbled backwards against a desk, and the class gasped in unison. *Don't you come near my son again*, the man said, and Mr. Franklin heard the door slam shut. Someone—a student—helped him up, and someone else—a girl—pressed the intercom and said, *Send security! Something's happened in room 315!*

The man was Dave Renton, James' father. James and two other boys had accused him of unwanted sexual advances. But what had he ever done? Patted James' shoulders, perhaps, called him 'Jimbo,' and maybe once mussed his hair, offhandedly, a reward for a job well-done. It was no different from how he treated other students. Mostly. He was put on paid administrative leave, and Dave was charged with battery. The next morning, a radio station called Dave Renton "father of the year." "We need to rid our schools of sexual predators," said the DJ. "If it had happened to my son, I'd have done the same thing." Even after James recanted—he was just going along with his friends' revenge plot—his career in Chicago was over. Students shied away as though he carried a taint. In the halls, he heard them whisper: *Perv. Faggot.* It was as if he were still in high school himself. Even the statements of support seemed wan in the face of the names, the threats, the punch. Marcia bit back her silence—"I know you didn't do it," she said—but there was a crinkle in her smile that suspected, that would always wonder. "I never would have"—he said—"not with a student." And while the statement was true, he could never make it sound definitive.

But that was history now, and Richard was an outstanding assistant. He rinsed test tubes with distilled water and replaced the flints in the lighters without being prompted. He straightened and organized the shelves of the storeroom, separated the combustibles from the flammables, and tightened the seals on the ether bottles so hard that Mr. Franklin had difficulty opening them. He seemed more energetic than Mr. Franklin had ever seen him previously, even though in class itself, he was as withdrawn as ever. He had raised his hand to answer a question once, and Mr. Franklin had pointed to him, but Brad Jeffers jumped in, as if intercepting a pass.

Mr. Franklin stopped going to the pool at all, and when he had nothing for Richard to do, they'd dip into more advanced topics: organic chemistry, physical chemistry. Mr. Franklin admired Richard so much that he allowed him to grade Earth Science quizzes—the most thankless task imaginable. And before Richard left for the bus each day, he made sure that the gas valves on the lab desks were turned all the way off. *If it weren't for him*, Mr. Franklin thought, *this place would have blown up a hundred times by now.*

And this gave him an idea.

M R. FRANKLIN OUTLINED his plan to the administration for convincing otherwise apathetic students to take AP Chemistry. Explosions! The noisier, the better. A magic show-type assembly for the juniors and seniors. Hydrogen-filled balloons, flash paper, alcohol fires burning furious and ephemeral: all tricks of the trade. The administration seemed skeptical that he'd be able to pull the show together in two weeks, but he emphasized that it was a matter of getting the materials. Privately, he knew how hesitant distributors were to send flammables to this area, where militias and meth labs sprouted like mushrooms after rain.

But work started immediately, and Mr. Franklin used Richard for all he was worth. On afternoon, he drew an equation on the board for Richard to solve: cellulose and nitric acid on the left, the right side blank, an open question. Richard saw the equation the moment he walked in. He knew this was some sort of test. "Those hydroxyl clusters," Richard said, "they become ester nitrates, right?" He drew a wobbly nitrocellulose to the right of the equals sign, and at that moment, Mr. Franklin couldn't have been more proud.

That night, Marcia told him, "You're taking quite an interest in him."

"He seems lonely sometimes," he replied.

"Are you sure it's a good idea?"

"He's just lost. Needs a little guidance. Reminds me of me when I was his age. I don't think he knows what he wants from life."

"And do you know? What you want?"

"Of course I do." He put his head on Marcia's belly, listening for the baby underneath.

She lifted her hand as if to pat his head, but it hovered an inch above making contact. "I meant, at sixteen."

He couldn't hear the baby over Marcia's burbling intestinal gases. She was due in less than a month. "I had a good idea," he said.

"Did you?" It was a question, not a challenge. He had no reason to resent it, but did anyway.

"Obviously, I didn't know every single step. But it got me—" The end of the sentence should been *where I am today*. But he couldn't say it.

"Well, you're going to be a great father."

Perhaps. But he wasn't Richard's father. If he were, he would have told Richard to stand up straight, not to shuffle his feet in the hallways, to ignore what the other students said. He would have said that he, too, had lived through it, that he'd wanted to give up hundreds of times: when he missed an easy lay-up in gym class; when he went up before Speech class with sweat blackening his armpits; when he realized that his clothes were the wrong color, the wrong style, the wrong year.

But things have changed, Richard would say.

Let me tell you something, he'd say. *These names that people call you—I've been called the same thing. I got pushed against the lockers, shoved in the halls. I would come home with bruises on my shoulders, and my father would say 'So why don't you do something about it?' And I did. I tamped down all those feelings—anger, pain, fear—until they had broken off into a nub. I lived through it. And so will you.*

And Richard would nod, think it through. *Thanks*, he'd say.

Sure, Mr. Franklin would respond, and give him a hug.

T HREE DAYS FROM the Chemistry Magic! show, Mrs. Okrina, the assistant principal, paid him a visit.

"Joe," she said, chidingly passive-aggressive, "you haven't been doing your attendance sheets correctly."

The sheets were Scantrons, a bubble for absent, a bubble for tardy. It was an insult to say that they hadn't been filled out properly.

"Are you sure?" he asked.

"I just noticed a discrepancy, that's all." Her print-out showed that, for the last two weeks, Richard had been absent from every class except for chemistry. He remembered Richard in class just that morning, wearing a gray polo fraying along the collar, and for a moment, Mr. Franklin thought that something was indeed wrong with the Scantron sheets. Maybe something all the other teachers were doing?

He didn't tell Mrs. Okrina this. He said he'd be more careful.

Just before Richard came in for seventh period, Mr. Franklin set the tray of flash paper and guncotton they had made the day before. Richard had been scrupulously careful, filling the ice bath until his fingers were red from cold. He blended the nitric and sulfuric acids with the glass stir stick and held the paper in the solution with tweezers, firm and secure, despite thick safety gloves.

On another desk, Mr. Franklin prepared a Bunsen burner. He

attached the rubber hose to the spigot and double-checked the seal. He kept the flame low, a blue flicker, a whisper of fire. Should he be disturbed or pleased that Richard came only to his class? *Where did he spend his day?* Surely the librarians would have noticed him sitting all day, wandering the stacks, running his finger along the books' spines. But Mr. Franklin knew that probably wasn't the case. In his own high school days, he could stay hidden when he wanted: in a bathroom stall with his feet propped up against the door or in the sound booth twenty feet above the auditorium stage. Even now, he had the pool, the solitude he'd given up for Richard. And now Richard had gotten him in trouble—a very minor trouble, but trouble all the same.

Richard came in, slouching as always. But when he saw the tray, he shrugged off his backpack and dropped it to the floor. His shoulders straightened, and a smile crept across his face.

"Is that it? Is it dry?"

Mr. Franklin nodded. "Go check it out." He should have been angry, but couldn't keep it mustered.

Richard rolled a piece of cotton between his fingers. "Feels kind of damp," he said.

"It still has three days to dry. But the paper is ready."

Mr. Franklin held a sheet the size of a dollar bill. It felt ready to crumble.

"Watch this," he said.

He lit a wooden stirrer atop the Bunsen burner and brushed the flame against a corner of the paper. It burst into light, bright enough to blind, and then he was holding only a wisp of smoke in his hand.

"Cool," said Richard, and Mr. Franklin could tell that he meant it. Mr. Franklin blew out the flame on the stick. The wood smoldered.

Okay. He'd have to confront Richard at some point. He cleared his throat.

"Why aren't you going to any of your other classes? Mrs. Okrina came to me—"

But before he could finish, Richard waved his hand, as if to say *No more.*

He continued: "I just don't understand why—"

"It's none of your business," Richard said. "I mean, why should you care?"

"I'm concerned, that's all."

"Oh. You're concerned. Everyone's concerned. All anyone ever does is talk about how concerned they are."

It was true. Mr. Franklin brimmed with clichés: *You're throwing away a bright future. You've got your whole life ahead of you.* He was an Afternoon Special, a buffoon. He'd heard the same things, and they hadn't helped any. What sort of life did Clarkfield offer either of them? This rural bear trap, this shithole. He put his hands on Richard's shoulders, a gesture of exhaustion, of resignation. He wanted to say, *If you've given up, I've given up, too.* "Richard," he said, "tell me what you want."

"What I want..." Richard said. He looked at the floor, at his hands, then to the tray of flash paper. He took a sheet and tossed it out over the burner. It flared and disappeared before Mr. Franklin could stop him. He turned to Mr. Franklin, his head tilted slightly, as if wondering if there was any good way to answer the question. Richard hung limp in his hands, and Mr. Franklin wanted nothing more than to bring him close and breathe life into him.

WHAT HAPPENED NEXT remained a matter of speculation. The administration accepted what Mr. Franklin told them. He'd been careless. He should have double-checked to make sure the guncotton was completely dry before touching it to the flame and throwing it into the air. The cotton caught fire instead of flaring out, and it fell onto his moustache. He ran to the face wash, hit the paddle, and the spurting water extinguished the fire. And then he'd blacked out.

The story among the students, however, was that Richard was the one who set fire to Mr. Franklin's moustache. They said that Richard had been planning to blow up the school, and had befriended Mr. Franklin just enough to be able to open all the gas nozzles at once, and that Mr. Franklin had walked in on the plot and averted disaster, and that's when Richard torched Mr. Franklin's face. *That guy was weird*, they said. *Antisocial. There was something wrong with him.*

There had been a fire, true, but Richard wasn't the cause. With his arms still on Richard's shoulders, Richard had stepped forward, that was true, close enough so that he could feel Richard's breaths on his chin, the hot bursts, the sourness. He saw the wisps of hair sprouting on Richard's own upper lip, and Mr. Franklin had thought that, maybe, if he'd had a Mr. Franklin when he was Richard's age, things would have been different. And when he kissed Richard, he felt the bristles of his moustache compact, and Richard didn't pull away, not immediately—and when he did, he stared at Mr. Franklin the way Marcia sometimes did, as if they knew him better than he knew himself. And Richard realized something—Mr. Franklin saw it take shape on his face, the moment when the world snaps into shape—and Richard fled the room, knocking the rubber hose loose from the spigot in his haste. Mr. Franklin—horrified, frightened, but most of all exhausted—collapsed onto one of the lab bench stools. The hiss of gas blew on his face. And then—he could never figure out where it came from, or why—and then there was a spark.

While still in the hospital, Mr. Franklin learned that Richard had run away. Marcia told him, sitting next to his hospital bed, knitting—baby booties? A scarf? He couldn't tell. He patted his face; the gauze circling his head pressed against his upper lip. The taste of charred flesh lingered in his mouth, sickeningly sweet, and the smell of burned keratin lingered in his nostrils. He wanted to lick his lips, but it hurt through the painkillers. Richard had stolen his parents' car and ditched it in Minneapolis. He was gone—as irrevocably as Mr. Franklin's moustache. All that remained was the searing sensation of Richard's lips against his, a moment so ephemeral that it could have been inscribed on flash paper.

You fool, he wanted to say to Richard. *It was only another year before you graduated. You would have lived through it.*

I could have, Richard would say. *But then what happens after that? Tell me. Tell me what happens next, Joe.*

And Richard would watch Mr. Franklin's lips carefully. The moustache was no longer there to hide his words, and Richard would wait patiently for a response.

CONTRIBUTORS

BRENT ARMENDINGER is the author of *The Ghost in Us Was Multiplying*, a book of poems forthcoming from Noemi Press in 2014. He has also published two chapbooks, *Archipelago* and *Undetectable*, and his work has appeared in many journals, including *Aufgabe, Bateau, Bombay Gin, Colorado Review, Denver Quarterly, LIT, Puerto del Sol, RECAPS Magazine, Volt,* and *Web Conjunctions*. In 2013, Armendinger was a resident at the Headlands Center for the Arts. He teaches creative writing at Pitzer College and lives in Los Angeles. His favorite flower is the purple lilac.

SALLY BELLEROSE is a novelist, poet, and retired RN. Her novel *The Girls Club* (Bywater Books, 2011) won several awards including a Prose Fellowship from the NEA. Sally is working on a linked story collection about old ladies behaving badly titled *Fishwives* . The title story from the collection won the 2011 Saints and Sinners Award. A selection of Sally's poetry can be found in *Lady Business: A Celebration of Lesbian Poetry* (Sibling Rivalry Press, 2012). Her poems and prose usually involve themes of sexuality, illness, and class. Her favorite LGBT writers include Joan Nestle, James Baldwin, Emma Donoghue, and Jeanette Winterson. Love-Lies-Bleeding is the favorite flower in Sally's garden.

JAMES CIHLAR is the author of the poetry books *Rancho Nostalgia* (Dream Horse Press, 2013), *Undoing* (Little Pear Press, 2008) and the chapbook *Metaphysical Bailout* (Pudding House Press, 2010). His writing has been published in the *American Poetry Review, The Awl, Court Green, Smartish Pace, The Rumpus, Lambda Literary Review,* and *Forklift, Ohio.* The recipient of two Minnesota State Arts Board Fellowships for Poetry and a Glenna Luschei Award from *Prairie Schooner,* Cihlar teaches literature and publishing courses at the University of Minnesota in Minneapolis.

ELISE D'HAENE is the author of the novel *Licking Our Wounds* (Permanent Press), co-author of the erotic series *Red Shoe Diaries* (Penguin/ Berkeley Books), and has published several short stories, including "Married," winner of a Hemingway award. As a screenwriter her credits include *The Little Mermaid II* and Showtime's *Red Shoe Diaries.* She teaches screenwriting at Point Park University in Pittsburgh. Elise is praying for a renewed bounty of milkweeds in North America.

VIET DINH was born in Da Lat, Vietnam and fled the country on the next-to-last helicopter out of Saigon. He grew up in Aurora, Colorado and, as a young man, was influenced greatly by Denton Welch. He earned his BA from the Johns Hopkins University and his MFA from the University of Houston. He has received fellowships from the National Endowment for the Arts and Delaware Division of the Arts. His work has won an O. Henry Award and appears in numerous literary journals, including *Zoetrope: All-Story, Five Points, Fence, Threepenny Review, Michigan Quarterly Review, Black Warrior Review, Chicago Review, Epoch,* and *Greensboro Review.* He did not, however, write the Patriot Act. He loves peony bushes big enough to hide a cat under.

ZOE DONALDSON is a writer and editor living in Brooklyn, New York. Her work can be found in *Confrontation Magazine* and *O, The Oprah*

Magazine, where she is as an Assistant Editor. She's currently at work on a chapbook inspired by lesbian pulp fiction novels from the 1950s and 60s. "I would have to say Joan Larkin, Sarah Schulman, and Eileen Myles are three queer writers I couldn't do without. Favorite flower goes to the sunflower."

BLAS FALCONER is the author of *The Foundling Wheel* (Four Way Books) and *A Question of Gravity and Light* (University of Arizona Press). The recipient of an NEA Fellowship, the Maureen Egen Writers Exchange, and a Tennessee Individual Artist Grant, his poems have been featured by Poets and Writers, The Poetry Foundation, and Poetry Society of America. A coeditor of *Mentor and Muse: Essays from Poets to Poets* (Southern Illinois University Press) and *The Other Latino: Writing Against a Singular Identity* (University of Arizona Press), he teaches at the University of Southern California and in the low-residency MFA at Murray State University. Among the many inspiring poems by LGBT writers, Atsuro Riley's work keeps calling him back. His favorite flower is the thistle.

CELESTE GAINEY is the author of the full-length poetry collection, *the gaffer*, forthcoming from Arktoi Books. Her chapbook, *In the land of speculation & seismography*, was chosen by Eloise Klein Healy and published by Seven Kitchens Press as runner-up for the Robin Becker Prize. Right now she's fixated on the texture and spiky lilac blooms of mondo grass.

BENJAMIN S. GROSSBERG's books are *Sweet Core Orchard* (University of Tampa, 2009), winner of the 2008 Tampa Review Prize and a Lambda Literary Award, and *Underwater Lengths in a Single Breath* (Ashland Poetry Press, 2007). His third book, *Space Traveler*, is forthcoming from the University of Tampa press. "Queer writer who influences me: Whitman (Uncle Walt)." Favorite flower: Hibiscus.

J HARR is a transgender poet and writer. His one-act play *City of Iron* was performed in the Waterman Theatre in May of 2011. He is currently finishing his undergraduate degree in Creative Writing at Oswego State University, and is employed as a theatrical lighting designer. Favorite flower: Lilac.

CHARLES JENSEN is the author of a poetry collection, *The First Risk*, and several chapbooks, most recently *The Nanopedia Quick Reference Pocket Lexicon of Contemporary American Poetry*. His poems have appeared in *New England Review* and *Prairie Schooner*. He adores the fiction of David Leavitt and Douglas Coupland. Like Blair Waldorf, his favorite flowers are hydrangeas.

WAYNE JOHNS' poems have appeared in *Ploughshares, Image, New England Review*, and *Prairie Schooner*, among others. Reading: *Lookaway, Lookaway* by Wilton Barnhardt, and *We Disappear* by Scott Heim (was also re-reading Mysterious Skin--considering for a fiction into film course). Influences: would have to include the line that extends from Tennessee Williams and Carson McCullers to Jim Grimsley and Dorothy Allison. Favorite flower: depending on the day, gardenia or red spider lily.

JOY LADIN is the author of six books of poetry, including last year's *The Definition of Joy*, Lambda Literary Award finalist *Transmigration*, and Forward Fives award winner *Coming to Life*. Her memoir, *Through the Door of Life* was a 2012 National Jewish Book Award finalist. Her work has appeared in many publications, including *American Poetry Review, Prairie Schooner, Parnassus: Poetry in Review, Southern Review, Southwest Review, Michigan Quarterly Review*, and *North American Review*, and has been recognized with a Fulbright Scholarship. She holds the David and Ruth Gottesman Chair in English at Stern College of Yeshiva University. Favorite flower: Iris.

JOSEPH O. LEGASPI is the author of *Imago* (CavanKerry Press) and

Subways (Thrush Press), a chapbook. Recent works appeared in Poem-A-Day from the Academy of American Poets, *jubilat, diode, South Dakota Review, Stone-Water Review*, and the anthologies *Collective Brightness* (Sibling Rivalry Press), *Flicker and Spark* (Low Brow Press) and *Coming Close* (Prairie Lights/ University of Iowa Press). He co-founded Kundiman (www.kundiman.org), a non-profit organization serving Asian American poetry. His favorite flower is the peony.

ELEANOR LERMAN: "My favorite flower is the gladioli because it was my mother's and it reminds me of her. Jane Rule remains an important author in my personal list of writers who made a lasting impression on me; just by accident, when I was about eighteen, I found her book *This is Not For You* in a box of books that was being tossed out on Charles Street in the Village, where I lived at the time. I didn't have a lot of money, so free books were always a welcome gift. When I finally read Rule's book, it was a revelation because, except for the occasional allusion here and there, I had no real idea that there was anything like 'gay literature.' It was quite eye-opening for me and probably gave me a little push to change some of the pronouns in the poetry I had begun writing."

ROBIN LIPPINCOTT is the author of three novels—*In the Meantime, Our Arcadia*, and the Lammy-nominated *Mr. Dalloway*—as well as a short story collection, *The Real, True Angel*. His fiction and nonfiction have appeared in over thirty journals, including *The Paris Review, Fence, American Short Fiction, The Lumberyard, The New York Times Book Review*, and many others, all the way back to "Christopher Street." His essay here, "Piece of My Heart," will be published in the anthology *The Women We Love: A Gay Homage*, edited by Jason Howard (Cleis Press, 2014). Robin's latest book, *Blue Territory: A Meditation on the Life and Work of Joan Mitchell*, will be published by Typecast in May 2014. Gay male writers I admire: Edmund White, James Schuyler, Jamie O'Neill, Tony Kushner, Jean Genet, Tennessee Williams, Marcel Proust. Favorite flower: the sunflower.

PAULA MARTINAC is the author of three novels, including the Lambda Literary Award-winning *Out of Time*, which was recently re-released as an e-book. After 22 years in New York City, she now lives in Pittsburgh, where she works as a health/nutrition writer, editor and coach. She recently read and loved Jeanette Winterson's memoir, *Why Be Happy When You Could Be Normal?* and is (still) working on her own memoir-in-essays, *A Quarter Acre.* Her favorite flower is the iris, even though it refuses to grow in her garden.

JEN MEHAN holds an M.F.A. in Poetry from the University of Miami. She has edited various journals and magazines, served as an intern for the *Joe Milford Poetry Show*, and attended poetry classes at Georgia Tech and the Sarah Lawrence College Summer Seminars for Writers. She is an avid crafter, baker, and bookmaker.

ANGELO NIKOLOPOULOS is the author of *Obscenely Yours*, winner of the 2011 Kinereth Gensler Award (Alice James Books 2013). His poems have appeared in *Best American Poetry 2012, Best New Poets 2011, Boston Review, Fence, The Los Angeles Review, Tin House*, and elsewhere. He is a winner of the 2011 "Discovery" / *Boston Review* Poetry Contest and the founder of the White Swallow Reading Series in Manhattan. He teaches at Rutgers University and lives in New York City.

TRACY JEANNE ROSENTHAL is a pop culture parasite. Some of her writing is online. Some of it is stuck in fan mail to Rihanna or in hate mail to Lacan. Her first chapbook, *Close*, was just released with Sibling Rivalry Press. She likes orange lilies.

SAM ROSS's poems have appeared or are forthcoming in *Gulf Coast, Tin House, Indiana Review*, and others. His manuscript *Nights Not Knowing Where* was a finalist for publication in Copper Canyon's first open reading period, and he currently serves as the managing editor of *Circumference*, a journal of poetry in translation. He is currently reading Eileen Myles, Mark Bibbins, Tim Dlugos, and Hilton Als. Favorite flower, tulip.

PATRICK SAMUEL lives in Chicago where he received his MFA from Columbia College. Recently nominated for a Pushcart Prize, his work has appeared in *Juked, Columbia Poetry Review, BathHouse Journal, <kill author,* and *elimae.* Tulips are his favorite flower. Leland Hickman is the one queer writer who has mattered most to him.

ELAINE SEXTON is the author of two collections of poetry, *Sleuth* and *Causeway.* Her poems, reviews, and photography have appeared in numerous journals as wide ranging as *American Poetry Review, Poetry, Art in America, Sinister Wisdom*, and *You Are Here: The Journal of Creative Geography*! She teaches poetry and text and image workshops at Sarah Lawrence College.

KATIE JEAN SHINKLE is the author of one novel, *Our Prayers After the Fire,* forthcoming from Blue Square Press, and three chapbooks, most recently *Baby-Doll Under Ice* (Hyacinth Girl Press, forthcoming.) She is the Associate Editor of *Denver Quarterly.* Favorite flower: Velvet Queen Sunflower.

DANEZ SMITH, a Cave Canem Fellow and 2-time Pushcart Nominee, works in Madison, WI, as a Student Advisor for the First Wave Program at UW-Madison. He likes tattoos, bad food, drinking Capri Suns, reading manga and work from James Baldwin, Audre Lorde, Jericho Brown, & Sam Sax. His recent work appears or is forthcoming in *decomP, The Cortland Review, Anti-, Southern Indiana Review, Muzzle,* and other journal and anthologies. Favorite Flower: Black Calla Lilies.

WILL STOCKTON teaches Renaissance literature and queer studies at Clemson University. His book *Crush*, a collection of poems and essays co-written with D. Gilson, is forthcoming from Punctum Books. His favorite flower is the (Wild) Irish Rose.

ALEXIS STRATTON is a native of Illinois but has spent her life in many homes, from New Orleans to South Korea. She received an MFA in Creative Writing from the University of South Carolina and works as an educator for a non-profit organization in Columbia, SC. Her fiction has appeared in *Ayris Magazine, Bare Root Review, Breakwater Review*, and *The Drum Literary Magazine*.

Born in Seattle in 1979, **JULIE MARIE WADE** is the author of *Wishbone: A Memoir in Fractures* (Colgate University Press, 2010), winner of the Lambda Literary Award in Lesbian Memoir, and *Postage Due* (White Pine Press, 2013), winner of the Marie Alexander Poetry Series. Julie lives with her partner and their two cats in Dania Beach and teaches in the creative writing program at Florida International University.

HILARY A. ZAID holds an A.B., summa cum laude, in English and American Literature from Harvard and a Ph.D. in English Literature from Berkeley. Francine and Ellen are the protagonists of her first novel *Paper Is White*, excerpts from which have appeared in *Skin to Skin* and *Cactus Heart*. Current favorite queer writers: Lori Ostlund's *The Bigness of the World* (her Flannery O'Connor award-winning collection) and Hilary Sloin's quirky spoof of the 80s art scene *Art on Fire*, as well as the cross-genre lyric non-fiction of queer writer Maggie Nelson. Hilary lives with her spouse and two sons in Oakland, California. She does not have a cat. Favorite flower: tulips in February.